The Serpent and The Wolf

Chapter 1

The dense fog effortlessly rolled down the hill and
settled onto the battlefield. A lone figure stepped
out of the tree line and surveyed the carnage.
Bodies of men, women and horses covered the
blood-soaked ground. Fires from the previous
battle still burned in the distance. Harold looked
up and saw vultures circling overhead.

A great army gathered behind their Viking
commander and began hitting the front of their
shields with their battle axes. Their bravado was

cut short when a defining roar echoed across the valley and an ominous silhouette made its way through the fog. The warriors were silent. The commander unsheathed his sword and held it up high when the dragon's head pierced the fog. The beast roared, flames erupting from its mouth.

Harold pointed his sword at his adversary and yelled, "No mercy!" He took one step forward, and his helmet and wig fell off his head and landed on the ground.

"Cut, cut!" the director yelled. He mumbled as he wiped the sweat from his beard. "I went to film school for this shit?"

"Hey, this shit pays you well, so don't complain, Spielberg," Chad said to the recently graduated filmmaker.

"Sorry," Harold said, picking the wig and helmet off the ground.

"What the hell?" the director mumbled. "I was supposed to be making Oscar-worthy movies, not this crap." He half-heartedly smiled at Harold. "Not your fault, Harry. It's my crack makeup department."

"Screw you, Ricky!" the director's sister yelled.

"Jesus Christ, Thelma, get something to hold that stuff in place," the director barked.

"The bobby pins aren't working. What else do you want me to do? I can't help it if he has thin hair!"

"I don't care, use velcro if you have to!"

"Thin hair? Velcro?" Harold said.

Chad walked over and stood in front of Harold. "You have a lion's mane, bro. Don't worry about it."

"Seriously, don't you think this is a bit much for an attorney commercial?" Harold asked.

"No way, you look like a Viking god, dude," Chad replied. "Plus, we have to do this kind of stuff to compete with that jackass who swings a sledgehammer around and yells at the camera. Or the other moron that rides a motorcycle into people's houses. Go big or go home, right?"

"I guess," Harold half-heartedly agreed. "What ever happened to just making sure the little guy had a voice and that he could have justice like the rest of us?"

"Unfortunately, those days are gone, my friend," Chad said, adjusting Harold's chain mail. "It's about money and winning now."

Harold knew Chad meant well. The two had been fraternity brothers and roommates in college. Chad had gone on to get his MBA while Harold went to law school and now, they were business partners in several ventures.

The two were complete opposites but meshed well together. Whereas Chad was boisterous and rubbed some people the wrong way, Harold was more subdued and analytical. The same went for their appearance. Harold had a tall, athletic build, dark hair and crystal blue eyes. On the other hand, Chad was short, stocky, bald most of his life, and sweated a lot. However, Chad recently had hair plugs put in and now had a glorious head of hair.

"Everybody take five!" Rick yelled into his bullhorn. He looked over at his assistant. "Marty, tell the extras to get up and move around before the vultures come down and start pecking at them."

"Will do, boss," Marty replied, giving Rick a thumbs up.

"Oh and Marty."

"Yeah, boss?"

"Tell the effects guys to get the dragon ready for another take."

"Gotcha, will do, boss."

Harold's assistant, Beatrice, scrolled through the schedule on her phone. "Oh no," she gasped when she saw the time. "Harry," she said, power walking over to him and Chad.

The two of them looked up at her as she approached.

"Hey, we're trying to make dreams come true here," Chad barked.

"Easy," Harold said. "We'd be lost without her," he sternly mumbled to Chad.

Beatrice looked down at her feet when she heard a squishing sound. Her shoe sank into the mixture of fake blood and mud, up to her ankle. "Damn it, these are new shoes," she said, pulling her foot up from the ooze.

Chad laughed at first, but then looked down at his feet. "Shit, my boots," he said.

Harold momentarily chuckled when Chad went into a profanity-laced tirade about how much he paid for his boots. He looked up at Beatrice. "What's up, Bee?"

Beatrice had a look of horror and disgust on her face when she looked at her ruined shoe. She quickly regained her composure and came back to reality. "You have to be in court in thirty minutes, Harry."

"What?" Harold blurted out.

"Whoa, whoa, whoa, we spent a lot of money on this," Chad said, gesturing towards the commercial set. "We can't just shitcan it."

"I can't be late, this judge is a real hard ass," Harold said, pulling the chain mail shirt over his head.

"Alright, go. I got this," Chad said.

"Thanks, bro, I owe you," Harold said, handing his sword and shield over to Chad. He looked to Beatrice. "Let's go. I'll change while you drive." They ran past the film crew and toward Harold's old 4Runner.

"Hey, wait," Rick said as they ran past him. "Where are you going? We're not done here." He turned around and glared at Chad. "What the hell, dude?"

"We're still a go," Chad reassuringly said. He pulled the chain mail shirt over his head and slid his arms in. Then, he pointed at Thelma. "Alright sweetheart, you won't have any trouble getting that helmet to stay with this fine work of art," he said referring to his newly bought locks.

"Pendejo," Thelma mumbled as she walked over to him.

Rick watched Beatrice and Harold race off down the dirt road. The large all-terrain tires threw up a cloud of dust in their wake. The aspiring director turned around and marched over to Chad. "This won't work, Chad. You don't look like Harry at all."

"Listen up, Ridley Scott, we're going to make this work," Chad growled. "Use CGI or whatever you have to and let's finish this. Okay?"

"CGI?" Rick asked. "We don't have the budget or access to that stuff!"

"I'll give you an extra grand if we pull this off. Deal?" Chad's negotiating skills were second to none.

At first, Rick was dumbfounded but quickly regained his composure. "Well, I guess I can play around with camera angles and some other tricks."

"That's the spirit," Chad said with a jester's grin. He looked at the extras sitting on the ground. "On your feet, gentlemen. We're slaying a dragon today." He unsheathed his sword.

"Whatever," Rick mumbled, walking back behind the camera. "I should've gone to med school."

Chad took in a deep breath and exhaled. "Woo, it's a good day to be alive!"

"Cue the dragon!" Rick yelled into his bullhorn. "Okay, action!"

"No mercy!" Chad yelled as he and his warriors charged across the field towards the mechanical dragon.

The tires screeched when Beatrice swung the 4Runner onto the paved highway.

"Hey!" Harold yelled from the back of the vehicle.

Beatrice glanced at the rearview mirror and saw Harold's bare bottom fly from one side to the other. "You need a tan," she said with a giggle.

"And you need to get me there in one piece," Harold shot back.

Several minutes later, Beatrice slammed on the brakes and abruptly stopped in front of the courthouse. She looked at her watch. "With five minutes to spare. Damn, I'm good." She looked back at Harold. "You need to give me a raise."

Harold climbed out of the back of the vehicle and ran over to the passenger side. "Well if we win this case, I'll give it to you," he said, adjusting his tie in the mirror.

Beatrice handed him his briefcase. "New tie?"

"Yeah. Too flashy?"

"Nah, it's right in line with the whole hobo theme," Beatrice replied. Harold was just about to run off when Beatrice spotted something. "Oh, your beard!"

"Huh?" was all Harold got out before she ripped it off his face. "Ouch!" Beatrice nervously smiled while Harold rubbed his cheek. "Man, that's good glue."

"Go," Beatrice said, "knock 'em dead, kid."

"Will do," Harold replied. He ran up the courthouse steps.

Inside the courtroom, the judge's patience was wearing thin.

"Your Honor," the defense attorney said. "I motion for a dismissal of all charges since Mr. Gustafson isn't present."

The judge peered at the attorney. "Dismissal? Please, denied. We will reschedule for a later date." The judge lifted his gavel up but before he brought it down, Harold barged into the courtroom.

"Sorry I'm late, Your Honor!" Harold yelled, making his way to the front of the courtroom.

"Glad you could join us, Counselor," the judge remarked sarcastically.

"My apologies, I was filming another commercial," Harold said, pulling paperwork from his briefcase.

"I can't wait to see it. I'm breathless with anticipation," the judge said. The defense attorney, along with others in the courtroom, giggled.

"Order," The judge demanded, striking his desk with his gavel repeatedly. The room grew quiet.

Harold sat down next to his client. "I didn't think you were coming," the little elderly man said.

"Sorry about that. I'm here now."

The old man stared at Harold's tie. "Where did you get that, Goodwill?"

"Yeah, how did you guess?" Harold responded.

The judge looked over at Harold. "Counselor, the floor is yours."

"Thank you, Your Honor," Harold said, standing up for his opening arguments.

Beatrice was nervously pacing in the hallway, just outside of the courtroom. She looked up when she heard a commotion at the entrance of the courthouse. "Idiot," she whispered when she saw Chad arguing with the deputies at the metal detectors. He was still dressed in full battle gear.

"Come on, guys, it's not a real sword. It's a movie prop," Chad said, dropping it to the floor.

"The chain mail too, Chad," one deputy said.

The other deputy shook his head. "Seriously, Chad, how in the hell did you think you were going to get that stuff in here?"

"I forgot I had it on, okay?" Chad said, placing the items in a large plastic bin. He began to move forward when one of the deputies spoke up again.

"Ah, ah, ah, the hair too, Chad." Both deputies broke out in uncontrolled laughter.

"Suck it, Reggie. This cost more than you make in a year," Chad said, storming down the hallway.

Beatrice giggled too.

"Any word yet?" Chad asked.

"Not yet," Beatrice said.

The courtroom door opened and people began filing out. Thirty seconds later, Harold and the elderly gentleman walked out together.

"Thank you so much, Harry. I really appreciate everything you did for my family and me." The man gave Harold a bear hug.

"You're welcome, Mr. Lozano. You guys won't have to worry about money ever again," Harold said with a satisfied smile. The two men shook hands. "Take care." The elderly man walked down the hallway and disappeared into the crowd.

"Well?" Beatrice asked.

Harold grinned at her. "You're getting a raise, Bee."

"Yes!" she yelled, jumping up and down.

"Great job, champ," Chad said, patting Harold's shoulder.

"How did the shoot go?" Harold asked.

"With some camera tricks and an extra thousand dollars, it'll work."

"Ouch, sorry," Harold said.

"If it brings in the business I think it will, that grand will be pocket change for us."

Beatrice looked at her watch. "Oh!" she said, handing Harold a sub sandwich and grabbing his briefcase from him. "The lecture is at seven." Before he could get a word out, she handed him a backpack. "Change of clothes."

"Thank you," Harold said.

"And your keys," Beatrice said, tossing them over.

Harold ran down the hallway.

"Is he still taking history classes?" Chad asked.

"Leave him be, he loves that stuff," Beatrice replied.

Chapter 2

Harold slowly crept around the parking lot in his 4Runner. "Wow, full house tonight," he mumbled, scanning for a vacant space. He and several other drivers circled the lot like sharks readying themselves for a feeding frenzy.

Suddenly, he saw two girls walking through the lot towards their vehicle. "There we go," he said, gripping the steering wheel tightly. The young ladies got into the car and pulled out of the space. Before the other sharks could react,

Harold slammed his right foot onto the gas pedal and the SUV bolted forward. He covered the ground quickly and his tires screeched as he slid into the spot.

"Watch it, dude!" one of the students on the sidewalk yelled as he and several others jumped to the side.

Harold sheepishly got out of the vehicle. "Sorry about that," he said with a wave.

One of the students recognized Harold from his commercials. "Hey, it's Harry the Hobo Lawyer!"

Another student commented, "He's a douche."

The young man next to her said, "No way, he's freakin' awesome." Some of the other students joined him when he began to chant, "Harry, Harry, Harry."

Harold just smiled and grabbed his backpack from the passenger seat. He closed the door and used his remote to lock the doors. He quickly merged into the human highway heading towards the main lecture hall in the history building. As soon as he walked into the building, Harold darted towards the nearest restroom to change out of his suit and into his casual clothes.

A group of young ladies was seated at a table close to the entrance. They were sharing notes and the day's campus gossip as they sipped their overpriced coffee. One of the girls recognized Harold on his journey to the restroom.

"Oh look," she said. "It's the guy from the commercials."

Wendy looked up from her notes. "Who?"

The girl pointed at Harold. "The guy from the crazy commercials. The Hobo Lawyer." Wendy gave her a blank stare. "You haven't heard of him or seen the commercials?"

"No," Wendy said. Wendy was there more for the sharing of notes rather than the daily gossip. However, she did find Harold attractive when she saw him.

"Oh. My. God. You have to see this," her friend said, opening her laptop. After a few clicks, she had one of the videos playing on her screen.

Wendy began watching. "Is he riding an elephant?" she asked in disbelief.

"Yep," her friend replied. "Here, check this one out."

Wendy giggled as she gazed at the screen. Harold was jousting in full armor. He stared at the screen. "No mercy!" he yelled before his horse sped towards another knight approaching. "Holy crap," Wendy said with a laugh.

"Just wait," her friend said.

Harold was knocked off his horse, but quickly popped up from the ground. "I may get knocked down, but I get back up and keep fighting for you!"

"No way," Wendy said with a smile. "Well, I'm a fan now."

"See, I told you," her friend said. The bell chimed for everybody to be seated for the lecture. "We better get in there."

Harold came out of the restroom wearing a plaid button down shirt, a beat up pair of jeans and sneakers. He paused for a bit when he saw the table full of young ladies looking and smiling at him. He immediately zoned in on Wendy. *Wow, she's beautiful,* he thought.

The girls stood up and walked into the auditorium. They were all attractive in their own way, but something about Wendy stood out above the others.

Harold walked in after getting a cup of coffee. The auditorium was filling up quickly and the only seats left were in the back two rows. He saw Wendy and her friends sitting towards the middle of the auditorium.

While the other girls were pulling their laptops out to take notes, Wendy looked back to see where Harold was sitting. *Oh, there he is,* she thought when she saw him sitting down in the last row.

Harold happened to be doing the same. He locked eyes with Wendy. *She's looking at me,* he thought. *Act natural, idiot.* Wendy smiled at him. "Yes, she digs me," he said, trying to hide his enthusiasm with an awkward smile back.

He saw that she was taking her notes the old-fashioned way like him, with a pen and notepad. He held up his to show her. She kept smiling as her eyes lighted up even more. *She really is stunning,* Harold thought.

Their flirtation was interrupted when the Dean of the History Department spoke into the microphone onstage. "Please find a seat and quiet down so we can get started." Once the buzzing stopped, she continued. "Tonight, we are

honored to have Dr. Armistead as our guest
speaker. Her background and knowledge on
ancient man and conflicts are second to none.
Please join me in welcoming her," the Dean said,
clipping her hands together.

The audience erupted in applause as Dr.
Armistead approached the podium. Harold had
read all of her books and was a huge fan of the
esteemed academic.

Even in her advanced age, the former college
swimmer was still in fantastic shape. She
adjusted the height of the microphone. "Thank
you, Dean, and all of you for the warm welcome."

Once the applause died down, she brought up
her first slide. It was the continent of Africa. "Ten
thousand years ago, around 8000 BC, a group of
hunters and gatherers was viciously slaughtered
in a coordinated attack by a rival group in Africa.
Specifically, in Nataruk, Kenya," Dr. Armistead
switched to the next slide.

Harold leaned forward in his seat taking in every
word she said. A student raised his hand. "Yes,"
Dr. Armistead said.

"I thought Neanderthals and earlier humans
attacked one another before that," the student
stated.

"You're right, they did," the PhD validated. "It occurred out of fits of rage or a spontaneous event. This incident is unique because it was the first time that a group planned and carried out a concerted, military-styled attack on a rival group."

"Oh," the audience said collectively.

"This wasn't a mere fight over food, it was calculated genocide for land and hunting grounds." She went to the next slide. "Now, take a close look at the skulls we found on our excavation." She pointed to a hole in a skull fragment. "This is blunt force trauma from a weapon at close quarters. This leads us to believe that the assailants waited and ambushed these unfortunate humans."

"Whoa," some of the students mumbled.

"They were merciless and spared nobody. They killed men, women and children," she continued.

After about an hour, the professor concluded her lecture. "Another round of applause for Dr. Armistead," the Dean said. "We're thrilled that she's going to hang around for another hour or so to sign copies of her latest book in the lobby."

Wendy chuckled when she saw Harold do a fist pump after what the Dean announced.

Harold quickly exited the auditorium and got his place in line. There were already twenty people ahead of him. *Where did she go?* he wondered as he looked for Wendy. She and her friends stepped in line about thirty people behind Harold.

"Think quick, smart guy," Harold mumbled. He began waving to get Wendy's attention.

"Is he waving at us?" one of Wendy's friends asked.

"Who?" another asked.

"Harry the Hobo."

Wendy heard that and immediately looked up the line of people. Each girl had a letdown when they pointed at themselves and Harry nodded no.

"I think he's waving at you," one of the girls said to Wendy.

Wendy pointed at herself and Harold nodded yes. Then he motioned for her to come up to join him in line.

"Go girl, go," the girls said at the same time pushing Wendy forward.

She slowly began walking towards Harold. As she approached, Harold was mesmerized by her deep auburn hair and brown eyes. Both she and Harold simply stared at each other for a few seconds and smiled.

"Hi," Wendy said, breaking the not-so-awkward silence.

"Hi," Harold said, holding his hand to shake hers.

"I'm Wendy."

"I'm..."

"Hey!" a student yelled. He was six people back from Harold. "No cutting."

"She's not," Harold reassured him. "I was holding my girlfriend a place while she went to the bathroom."

"Hey, you're the Hobo dude," the student said. "No problem, man."

"Girlfriend, huh? You haven't even told me your name yet," Wendy said with a smirk.

"Sorry, I'm Harold. It's really nice to meet you, Wendy." Harold was lost in her eyes.

"Nice to meet you too and thank you for the spot in line."

Harold collected himself. "Oh, I got a copy for you," he said, handing her a copy of Dr. Armistead's latest book.

"Thank you, that's sweet."

A group of young men walked by. They recognized Harold and yelled, "No mercy!"

"Wow, you are quite the celebrity," Wendy said.

"Yeah, the law gig pays the bills but this is my true passion," he said holding up the book.

"Dr. Armistead?" Wendy asked with a hint of sarcasm.

"Ha-ha, no. History," Harold replied. "I think that if we learn from our past, it'll help free us in the future. I know, dorky, right?"

"Not at all, I know what you mean."

"Next," the publicist barked.

Harold broke his trance and placed the book in front of Dr. Armistead. "I'm a huge fan."

The history scholar looked up and recognized Harold. "Hey, I know you. Your commercials are very entertaining. I like the historical slant you put in all of them. I'm a big fan of yours as well, Mr. Gustafson."

"Thank you," Harold said, after she handed the book back to him.

"And is this your better half?" Dr. Armistead asked. Both Harold and Wendy fumbled around with their words. Before they could answer the question, Dr. Armistead added, "You are a very handsome couple."

They both blushed but didn't argue with the good doctor. After Wendy got her signed copy back they took a few steps and looked at each other again.

"Well after what she said, we have to go out with each other," Harold said.

"It is a powerful endorsement from a very intelligent woman. I can't argue against it," Wendy added with a smile.

Harold's phone began to repeatedly vibrate in his pocket. "Excuse me, I'm so sorry, it might be work," he said, reaching into his pocket.

"No problem," Wendy responded.

Harold saw multiple missed calls and texts from Beatrice. Wendy's friends exited the line and were motioning for her to leave with them.

"Looks like we're leaving," she said, reaching over and picking up a napkin. She wrote her phone number on it and handed it to Harold. "Very few people have this number. Memorize it and then eat the napkin, okay?"

"Will do," Harold replied with a warm smile. He handed her a business card. "Way too many people have this number but use it anytime and I'll be there for you."

Wendy looked at the card. "Will do," she said, looking deeply into Harold's eyes.

"I'm really looking forward to seeing you again, Wendy." *Dork, I can't believe I just said that,* he thought.

"Likewise, Harold. I want to know everything about you and hold you." She gasped and placed her hand over her mouth. "Oh shit, did I just say that out loud? Wow, I feel stupid."

"Don't, I feel the same way."

"Come on, Wendy!" her friends yelled.

"Bye, Harold."

"Bye, Wendy."

He watched her walk over to her friends. As they headed towards the exit, Wendy looked back at Harold and smiled a few times. Harold watched her walk out and couldn't quit smiling himself.

His phone buzzed again. "Damn it, Bee. What the hell's going on?"

"Harry, I'm at the hospital. It's your uncle Alex, he's hurt bad. It's really a bad situation, you better come quick." Harold could tell Beatrice had been crying.

"Okay, on my way," Harold ran towards the parking lot. He leapt into his vehicle and sped off down the street.

Thankfully, the hospital was only fifteen minutes away. Harold made it there in half the time. As he ran towards the emergency room entrance, he peered through the glass doors and saw Beatrice and Chad speaking with Frederick, a police sergeant and close friend of theirs. The three of them quickly looked over when Harold ran in.

"What happened?" Harold inquired. "Where is he?"

"He's still in surgery, Harry," Beatrice said, stumbling with her words and tears.

Chad rarely showed his compassionate side, only his close friends and family saw his caring nature. He put his arm around Beatrice. "Come on, let's go get some fresh air," he gently said. As they passed by Harold, Chad whispered, "It's bad, bro."

Perplexed, Harold asked, "Fred, what the hell happened?" He gazed down the hall and saw two police officers guarding the door to the operating room.

"Come on, let's get a cup of coffee so we can talk in private." Fred had a look of concern on his face.

Fred was already a large man when he met Harold and Chad in college. But over the years of police galas and free food, he was now a very large man. However, he was still quick and agile for a man his size. Many criminals underestimated his speed and were definitely surprised when they were apprehended by the behemoth.

The two of them entered the cafeteria and each poured themselves a cup of coffee. They walked over and placed their cups by the register.

"How's it going tonight, Pete?" Fred asked.

"Pretty good, Fred," Pete said. He looked over at Harold. "What's up, Harry?"

"Hey, Pete," Harold responded.

Pete rang up the purchase. "Two fifty, gentlemen."

Before Harold could reach for his wallet, Fred gave Pete a five dollar bill. "Keep it," Fred said, walking towards the dining area.

"Thanks," Pete said, gratefully.

The two sat down and faced each other. Fred scanned the area to make sure they could speak openly without others hearing or interrupting them.

"Dude, your uncle might be facing some deep shit with this," Fred started.

"What the hell happened?" Harry asked.

"Here," Fred said, handing Harold his phone.

"Oh my god," Harold gasped, looking at the screen. "Who are these guys? What attacked them?"

"Those dipshits are local KKK. Your uncle took out the three dead guys on the ground. Go to the next one," Fred said. Harold swiped over to the next picture. "He broke this dude's arm after that guy put six rounds into your uncle. I guess he blacked out after getting shot so many times. Alex is one tough sumbitch, Harry."

Harold was speechless for a moment but regained his composure. "How's that possible? I mean, he's an old man who's almost completely blind." He swiped back to the carnage picture. "It looks like a wild animal attacked these guys." He pivoted the screen to Fred. "Look, this guy's throat is ripped completely out."

"I know, I know, but we have several witnesses, including the hillbilly that survived, that Alex tore those guys apart in a matter of seconds. One of them is a veteran and he said he's never seen anybody move like that, Harry. Not only is he tough as nails, but apparently he's a bad mofo on top of that," Fred said with some admiration.

"I mean, he fought in Vietnam with my dad, but this is barbaric, borderline inhuman," Harold said. "What prompted all of this?"

"Did your uncle ever mention the elderly woman who owns the florist shop on Fiji street?"

"No, why?"

"It looks like she and your uncle had recently met and started seeing each other," Fred said. "Well, with him being a black man and her being a white woman, it didn't sit well with some of the locals."

"You gotta be kidding me, we don't live in the Dark Ages anymore," Harold replied angrily.

"I agree, but some folks here don't think like we do. Case in point, these morons," Fred said, referring to the KKK members in the pictures.

"Okay, but that still doesn't tell me why this happened, Fred."

"Here, this is why," Fred said, handing the phone back to Harold.

Harold looked at the photo and was visibly shaken. "Oh, no."

"Yep," Fred said. "They hanged her." Harold stared at the photo and sign around her neck that said, *Race Traitor.* "Your uncle got wind of what happened and did all of that. Dude, all four of them were armed, but he swept through them hard and fast before the fourth guy filled him with lead."

"What happens now?" Harold asked.

"It's nothing personal, Harry, but you know the procedure. He's in police custody until we can sort all of this out. The fourth inbred is under arrest and will be charged with the death of Ms. Jaworski, and attempted murder of your uncle."

"Right," Harold agreed.

"However, if your uncle pulls through, he's going to be charged with the deaths of the three KKK members," Fred added.

"That's bullshit, Fred!" Harold yelled.

"I agree with you, Harry, and I'm on your side. But the DA has a hard-on for this one, it's an election year. She wants to make a statement."

Harold stood up and pushed the chair back under the table. "I'm going to go see how he's doing."

"You can't see him, Harry," Fred said, standing up.

"What? Why?"

"No friends or family, only his legal representative," Fred said.

"DA?" Harold asked, already knowing the answer.

"Yep."

"I'll be his attorney and represent him," Harold fired back.

Before Fred could respond, the radio on his belt barked. "Hey Sarge."

Fred pushed the button on the side and spoke into the radio. "Yeah."

"He's out of surgery and they're moving him to a room."

"Roger that. His lawyer and I are on our way," Fred replied, winking at Harold.

"Thanks, man," Harold said.

"No problem. Let's go see what the doc says."

The two of them walked down the hallway and approached the two officers standing by the room.

"The doctor is in there now, Sarge," one of the officers said.

"Okay," Fred said. "Gentlemen, this is Mr. Corbin's attorney, Harold Gustafson. He can come and go as he wishes. Understood?"

"Yes sir," they both responded.

"Thanks again," Harold said, shaking Fred's hand.

"Let me know if you need anything."

After Fred walked off, Harold entered the room. The doctor who had operated on Alex was notating something in the chart while the two nurses checked the monitors.

The doctor looked up from the chart and over at Harold. "And you are?"

"Harold Gustafson. I'm his lawyer and nephew."

The doctor turned and looked at Alex lying motionless in his bed, then quickly back at Harold with a perplexed expression.

"Long story. My dad didn't make it back from Vietnam so Alex raised me as his own. He's been a close family friend for many years."

"Ah, gotcha," the doctor responded. The two nurses did their last checks and walked out of the room. "We've done all we can do for your uncle. It's up to him now if he pulls out of this or not."

"What are the odds, Doc?"

"About fifty-fifty, but he's a tough customer. He's in an induced coma right now so you won't get much response. But talk to him, he knows you're here." The doctor gave a sympathetic smile.

"Okay," Harold said, sadly.

The doctor paused by the door. "Your uncle has done a lot of charity work here at the hospital. We're all pulling for him, Mr. Gustafson."

"Thanks, Doc."

After the doctor walked out, the room was eerily quiet except for the heartbeat monitor. Harold quietly sat next to the bed and stared at Alex. He pulled out his phone to check his schedule for the next day.

Suddenly, Alex began to mumble incoherently. *I thought the doctor said he would be unresponsive,* Harold thought. He didn't understand what Alex was saying, but it was the same thing over and over. *What language was that?*

He began recording Alex with his phone. Harold stood up, leaned over and held the phone close to Alex's mouth. Alex repeated the phrase over and over. Harold's hand was down by the side of the bed, an inch away from Alex's hand. Alex slowly raised his pinky finger and gently touched Harold's hand with it.

Harold convulsed as if hit by lightning. He tried to pull away from Alex but he couldn't move or scream out in pain. He was quickly pulled away from the room. The floor and walls looked like dark streaks and smudges against a brilliantly lit tunnel.

His soul raced across space and time down the tunnel. It felt like he hit a brick wall when he stopped. Harold tried to catch his breath as he looked around. *What is this place?* he wondered.

The sky was gray and the air was frigid. Suddenly, something swooshed by his head. *What was that?* Before he found his answer, something hit him hard and threw him to the ground. A very large man with long hair and a beard leapt over Harold and slashed another large man across the chest. Steam rose from the chest wound as blood poured out and onto the ground next to Harold.

Is that a Viking?! Harold tried to regain his bearings. He looked around and saw giants engaged in battle. Harold was tall but these men made him look small.

The man that killed Harold's attacker looked down and stared at Harold. His hair, beard, face and chain mail were matted with blood and mud. His vibrant blue eyes looked like two beacons shining through a dark night.

Something grabbed Harold's shoulder and he was pulled again into the lighted tunnel. The wild men engaged in mortal combat disappeared. The air began to get hot and arid. His landing this time was a bit softer but not by much.

Harold shook his head. "Sand," he said as he watched the grains tumble from his hand and back to the ground. The bright sunlight made him squint. He coughed when the dust in the air invaded his throat and nostrils. *What's that?* He heard men yelling in the distance. *Arabic?* He saw a horde running towards him.

"Oh shit!" he yelled. The ground beneath him began to shake. The rhythmic galloping grew louder and louder. *French?* he wondered.

Within seconds, a horse and rider flew by him. He studied the rider. "A knight?" Then another and another. They charged towards the horde. One of the knights stopped next to Harold and looked down from his steed. The knight lifted his face mask and stared at Harold, his piercing blue eyes looking into Harold's soul.

"We will talk soon," the knight said.

Before Harold could say a word, something gripped his shoulder again and he was pulled away from the battle. Sights and sounds raced by his head as he soared across time and space. The air became cool again. Harold blinked and realized that he was now lying on a very cold patch of earth.

Joe Gregory

The sky was cold and gray again. The ground
was hard and unforgiving. The sounds of men
and machines at war echoed in the distance. He
started to rise to his feet when he heard a whisper
come from the pile of rubble right next to him.

"Stay down and keep quiet," the voice said.

A shot rang out from a building across the square.
The bullet struck the wall inches away from
Harold's head. Pieces of cement and dust rained
down on his head. A deafening boom exploded
from the rubble. Harold flinched and covered his
ears, which were now ringing from the decibel
overload. He saw a glass window shatter in the
far away building. It was deathly quiet again.

"Got him," the voice from the rubble said.

Harold looked over and realized he was lying next
to a concealed sniper. The only thing Harold
could see were his mesmerizing blue eyes.

"You need to be more careful, Harold," the voice
said.

How does he know my name? Before Harold
could mutter a word, he was pulled back into the
light. He began to hear the repetitive sound of the
heartbeat monitor. He came to a sudden stop and

was now back in the hospital room, standing next to Alex's bed.

He quickly pulled his hand away from Alex and took a giant step back.

"What the hell was that?"

Chapter 3

The next morning at the courthouse, Harold repeatedly went over every detail of the vision he had in the hospital room. *Was it stress? Fatigue? Someone or something sending a message to me?* He pulled his phone out and listened to Alex's voice.

"Wow, that's old Norse," came a voice from down the hall.

"What?" Harold uttered, quickly looking up.

"The voice," Wendy said, pointing at the phone. "And it's flawless, like an actual Norseman is saying it."

"How do you know that?" Harold asked, walking over and sitting next to Wendy.

"I'm working on my PhD on Nordic and Scandinavian Studies and Languages. I know, useless degree but I love it," Wendy said. "Hey, are you okay? You look beat."

"Yeah, long night. Can you translate this?" Harold asked, holding the phone up.

"Sure, play it again." Wendy listened intently to every word. Harold played it over again. She looked at Harold with a confused expression. "He's saying 'Father, why have you forsaken me?' over and over. Like I said, it's spoken perfectly. Who is he?"

"My uncle," Harold muttered.

"Really? Was he doing a reading or some kind of performance?"

"No, he's in a coma and said this while I was in his hospital room."

"I'm so sorry to hear that," Wendy said, grabbing Harold's hand. "What happened?"

"You probably saw the news about the hanging and KKK guys, right?"

"I did. Was your uncle one of the KKK guys?" Wendy asked awkwardly.

"Thankfully, no," Harold replied with some relief. "He was the African-American man that allegedly attacked them."

"He's your uncle?" Wendy asked.

"Long story."

"I have time," Wendy responded kindly.

"Speaking of, why are you here?" Harold asked.

"Speeding ticket. You?"

"I'm meeting the DA about my uncle."

"Tell me about him," Wendy said, nudging closer.

"My uncle Alex and my dad were best friends."

"Were?" Wendy asked.

"Yeah, my dad didn't make it back from Iraq."

"Sorry," Wendy said sympathetically.

"No biggie, it was a long time ago." Harold tried to put up a strong front, but Wendy could see the pain and sorrow in his eyes. "Uncle Alex and my dad were in the same unit. They were ambushed by the Vietcong. Both Alex and my dad were wounded in the fight. Somehow, my uncle Alex carried my dad out of the jungle but the medics couldn't save him."

"Wow," Wendy whispered.

"I know, right? Tough dude," Harold agreed. "He was awarded a bronze star and a purple heart, but it came at the cost of his eyesight."

"He's blind?"

"Not totally but pretty close," Harold said.

"How can an elderly blind man do all of that to a group of young skinheads?" Wendy asked in amazement.

"I don't know. That's why I took the case, so I can find out what the hell happened last night and why it happened."

"No kidding," she said. "Was he a language specialist or something in the military? Why does he know old Norse? It's an ancient language that's not really spoken anymore."

"I don't know," Harold replied with a sense of guilt. "I was always wrapped up with my own ambitions that I never really knew that much about my uncle. But no matter what, he was always there for me. See?" Harold showed her some of the pictures on his phone. "Here he is on the sideline when I was in pee wee football." He swiped to the next picture. "When I graduated college. And, when I got my law degree. He even helped me with my mom's passing."

Wendy was drawn to Alex's eyes. "Wow, he has beautiful eyes."

Harold looked at the picture. "Hmm, no kidding. I'd never noticed them before you said something." He looked up at Wendy. "See, I was a selfish asshole."

"Don't be too hard on yourself, Harry. We're all guilty of being self-centered when it comes to our ambitions, me included. Just keep going to the hospital and spending time with him. He knows when you're there."

"That's what the doctor said, too."

The door down the hall opened up. The DA's administrative assistant poked her head out. "Mr. Gustafson, she'll see you now."

"Thank you, I'll be right there," Harold said. He stood up and took a few steps towards the door, but stopped and looked back at Wendy. "Speeding ticket, right?"

"Yep, I have a lead foot."

He walked back and held his hand out. "I'll take care of that for you, but it'll cost you."

"Oh really? Remember, I'm a starving college student, Counselor."

"Just in case my uncle says anything else in an ancient, unused language, I'll need a translator. You'll be part of my legal team representing him."

"Wow, sounds important," Wendy said with a smirk.

"Oh, it is. And, you have to have dinner with me," Harold added. "Need some time to think about it?"

"Nope, you have a deal, Counselor," Wendy said with a glowing smile.

"Great!" Harold yelled a little loudly. He caught himself and covered his mouth with his hand. "Oops."

Wendy chuckled.

"I have to go but I'll notify the DA and the police department that you're on my team. You'll have full access. Meet me at the hospital later tonight?"

"I'll see you there," Wendy said. After Harold entered the office, Wendy walked down the hallway and exited the courthouse. "Cool," she mumbled with smile.

Harold's euphoria was short-lived when he saw the DA's facial expression. *Uh oh, she looks pissed,* he thought.

"Have a seat, Harry," she said sternly.

"Yes ma'am," Harold responded politely.

"I'm giving you fair warning, I'm going after everybody on this one, your uncle, those white supremacist idiots, everybody."

"But Susan—" Harold tried to interject.

"But nothing, Harry. It's an election year and I need a body count to appease the voters. This case is perfect because it'll appeal to both sides of the table." Harold tried to get another word in but she wasn't having it. "Full speed ahead. Prepare yourself for a dog fight, Harry."

"Yes ma'am, will do," Harry said stiffly, standing up and reaching over to shake her hand.

The DA gripped his hand firmly and looked him in the eye. "You're used to chasing money for your clients but now you're in my domain. We fight for lives in this arena. I'll see you in court, Counselor."

Harold's anger spiked over her using his uncle for political gain. She saw the rage in his eyes. "Damn right, you will, Susan." He released her hand and walked out of her office.

Chapter 4

Harry approached the two police officers guarding his uncle's hospital room. "Hey guys, how's it going?" He had his hands full carrying a large tray with four cups of fresh hospital coffee and four sandwiches.

"Hey, Harry," they responded.

"These are for you," Harry said, handing each officer a cup of coffee and a sandwich.

"Thanks," both officers replied. One of the officers smiled. "Bribery will get you everywhere." The other officer laughed.

Harry smiled. "My assistant, Wendy Gleichenhaus, will be here in a few minutes, she's on my legal team. Please let her in, okay?"

"Cool, no problem, Harry," one of the officers said in between chews.

"Thanks again for everything guys," Harry said before he entered the room. One of the nurses was checking the readings on the monitors. "Hey, how's he doing?" he whispered. He gently placed the remaining two cups of coffee and sandwiches on the table by the bed.

"Hey, Harry. No need to whisper, you're not going to wake him up," the nurse said. "He's been quiet but doing well.

"True, good point," Harold said.

The nurse studied Harold. "You look beat. You need to get some rest, too. Take care of yourself, Harry."

"You're right, I will."

"I'll be back in an hour to take more readings," the nurse said, heading for the door.

"Okay, thanks." Harold watched her walk out. He sat down in the chair by the bed. "Hey, Uncle Alex, it's me, Harry." Harold rubbed his own temples. "I hope you can hear me. I wanted to thank you for everything you've done for me. You were always there, no matter what. I was so caught up in making money and having more stuff, that I forgot to tell you how much I appreciate you." Harold wiped his eyes. "Hey, on a brighter note, I met a great girl, she'll be here in a few minutes. I know you're going to like her."

Harold's eyelids began to get heavy, the stress and lack of sleep were catching up to him. He jumped when he saw something out of the corner of his eye.

"Oh shit," he mumbled when he saw a large gray wolf sitting three feet away from him. *Stay calm, no sudden movements,* he thought.

It was easily the largest wolf he had ever seen, about Harold's height at the shoulders, standing on its four legs. Thankfully, it was calm and didn't seem to want to eat Harold. Its eyes stared into Harold's soul. One was as black as a moonless night. The other, white as untouched snow.

The enormous canine stood up and walked over to the door. It stopped, looked back at Harold and motioned with its head to follow it out.

"You want me to go with you?" Harold asked. The wolf nodded. *Holy crap, it understands what I'm saying.*

Harold walked over and stood next to it. The door opened on its own and the two walked through it at the same time. A cool, fresh breeze hit Harold's face. He looked around and, through a fog, saw that they were now walking on a dock towards a large object in the water.

The fog began to subside and a vessel became more clear with each step. "Whoa," Harold uttered when he saw the large dragon head on the bow of the boat. The wolf jumped from the dock onto the boat with ease. It turned around and looked at Harold.

"I take it you want me to come aboard?" he asked the wolf. It nodded. "Okay…" Harold nervously stepped onto the deck of the boat.

The boat pulled away from the dock. There was no crew, nobody rowing, just Harold and the wolf. But somehow, the boat effortlessly glided across the water. *How is this possible?*

The vessel quickly picked up speed heading down river. Harold scanned his surroundings and was in awe of the natural beauty. The water was crystal clear. He looked over the side and could see fish swimming below the boat. Then, he gazed up at the majestic mountain peaks that surrounded the valley. Their snow-capped peaks disappeared into the clouds. The trees and vegetation were lush and full.

Harold watched the wolf raise its head, enjoying the wind and sea spray hitting its face as they entered the open ocean. Soon, the land disappeared on the horizon and the waves grew larger now. Harold started to get an uneasy, queasy feeling from the motion. He ran to the side and leaned over the rail. After he was done vomiting, he looked at the wolf as he tried to regain his composure. The wolf was unfazed by the rough seas. It continued looking ahead, over the incoming swells.

Harold wasn't an expert navigator, but he knew they were heading north when he saw the sun setting in the west. Soon, the sun was chased away by the night. Harold watched the moonlight dance on the waves. He had been nauseous all day and felt another bout coming on. He crawled back over to the rail and hung his arm and head over the side again. The wolf looked back and quickly ran over to him.

"Oh shit, don't eat me!" Harold yelled, curling up in the fetal position.

The wolf bit down on his jacket and tossed him to the middle of the boat. Harold looked up and saw some kind of serpent spring out of the ocean and bite down on the side of the boat he had just been leaning on. The serpent released its vice-like grip and hissed at the wolf. The boat shook when the wolf growled back. Harold felt it deep in his chest.

The wolf was now between Harold and the serpent. The serpent slithered back and forth, trying to get a good look at Harold. But the wolf mirrored each movement, frustrating the sea beast. The monster let out a bloodcurdling scream and sank back into the dark waters. The wolf, satisfied that the beast was gone, turned and looked at Harold.

"Thank you," Harold said sheepishly.

The wolf bowed its head once and made its way back to the bow. Exhausted from the events of the day, Harold soon fell fast asleep.

The next morning, Harold was awoken by a repetitive and annoying sound. Still lying on his side, he cracked open his eyes and saw two large ravens perched on a log right next to him.

"Oh my gosh, will you two be quiet!" he yelled, frantically looking for something to throw at his hecklers. He quickly sat up and realized he was on land. "Where's the boat?" he asked. "Where's the wolf?"

The air was cold and crisp. The sky was calm and gray. The beach was covered in dark sand. It was just him, the log, and his two new companions. "Where am I?" he asked, taking in the rugged beauty of the mountains surrounding him. A soft white snowflake fell from the monotone sky and landed on his nose. Then another and another until millions began covering the ground. "Great," he said sarcastically.

The two ravens cawed incessantly and hopped back and forth on the log to get Harold's attention. He tried to ignore them but failed. "What?" he said, staring at the birds angrily. One of the birds flew over to the tree and landed on a branch. Harold rose to his feet and walked over. As he got closer, he could see that there were animal furs hanging on the branch.

As he reached over to pull one of the furs from the branch, the other raven flew over and joined his companion on the branch. Harold held the fur up and saw a hole cut out in the middle. He looked over at his new helpers. "My head goes through here?"

Both ravens cawed.

Harold slipped his head through and draped the skin over his shoulders and torso. "Ah, nice and warm." He looked over at the ravens and realized they were there to help. "Thank you. Sorry I was being a dick to you guys."

Both birds bowed their heads and cawed. One of the birds pointed to the ground with its beak. Harold gazed down and saw a pair of boots. "Oh, okay," he said, sliding them on, one by one. After he tied the belt around the fur to keep it tight against his torso, he asked, "Now what?"

The ravens took off and flew down a path through the tall trees away from the beach. Harold trusted his new pals now and followed them down the path. Very few snowflakes made it past the canopy of the mighty trees of the dense forest. The terrain was rocky and unforgiving. Harold had to watch his every step. The stones along the path were slippery and sharp.

Harold looked ahead and saw the two ravens sitting quietly on a branch. "What's up?" he asked, standing under them. Both birds looked down but didn't mutter a sound, they were completely silent. Harold got the hint that he needed to be quiet as well.

Suddenly, a large man stood up from the base of a tree in the distance. He pulled his trousers up and tied them off in the front. *That's a big dude,* Harold thought. *Wait a minute, that's the guy in my vision.* Harold couldn't forget his piercing blue eyes.

The large man was easily four to five inches taller than Harold, and built like a mountain. His long hair and beard went down to the middle of his chest and back.

The mountain man yelled. "Henrik!"

"What?" a voice said from some trees about fifty yards away.

"I found your sword!"

"Good, I'm coming."

Harold saw another man coming down the path towards the man by the tree. He was slightly smaller, Harold's size, with long dark hair and radiant blue eyes.

"Where is it, Ulfr?" the smaller man asked.

The large man pointed at the tree. "There at the base of that tree, under those branches."

Henrik drove his hand through the branches and felt something warm and squishy. A giggle slipped out from Ulfr. Henrik raised his hand to his nose and smelled the brown substance on his fingers.

"Is that shit? Your shit?" Ulfr burst out in laughter, pushing Henrik to the ground and running off down the path. "You ass!" Henrik yelled and he jumped to his feet. "I'm going to cut you from balls to throat when I catch you!" Henrik took off and chased Ulfr.

"Wow, those guys are big and fast," Harold whispered in admiration.

Both ravens took off and flew down the path after the men. Harold didn't move for a few seconds but realized that he better follow his two tour guides. After about a mile or so, Harold came to an opening just outside the forest. He saw Ulfr and Henrik wrestling in the snow and mud in front of a small, quaint abode.

"By the gods, what is going on out here?" an old man asked as he stepped out of the house.

Joe Gregory

He looked like an old warhorse with long gray hair and many scars on his face and arms. Harold could tell he had taken part in many battles; it showed on his face.

The old man was still strong enough to manhandle the two younger men. He reached down, grabbed both men and pulled them to their feet. "What are you two doing?" he asked them. Before they could answer, he smelled something rank in the air. "Is that shit?"

"Yes father, it is. It's Ulfr's shit," Henrik answered. Ulfr couldn't stop laughing. "He covered his shit with branches and said my sword was there."

"Ulfr," the old man said, looking at the larger man with some disappointment.

"I'm going to gut him, father!" Henrik yelled.

"Enough!" the old man yelled. "Ulfr, apologize to your brother."

"I'm sorry, brother," Ulfr said with a small giggle.

"Henrik, go wash up. Ulfr, collect our weapons. We're going to go see the Earl," the old man said.

"Yes, father," Henrik reluctantly answered and walked off.

The old man looked at his other son. "Ulfr, I raised you boys to be warriors not animals."

"Sorry, Father," Ulfr said. He grinned at his father. "But you admit, it was funny."

His father shook his head. "Funny but disgusting," the old man said with a slight smile. "Go get ready, I want to be in town by nightfall."

"Yes, Father," Ulfr said, running off to gather his things.

Chapter 5

It was still daylight when Ulfr, Henrik, and their father, Gustav, reached the edge of town.

Gustav paused and looked at his sons. "Behave yourselves and don't drink too much mead." He pointed his authoritative finger at his boys. Ulfr started to complain, and he quickly added, "And don't chase the nobles' daughters."

"But, Father," Henrik chimed in.

"But nothing. I had to give the Earl two goats so you two wouldn't be sacrificed to Odin after our last visit," Gustav continued. "One of the nobles wanted your heads." The sons didn't have a retort. "Give me your word."

"You have my word," Ulfr said.

"Henrik?" Gustav asked.

"Okay, okay, you have my word, Father."

Gustav placed a hand on each of his son's shoulders. "Look around while I go let the Earl know we're here." He walked off and headed for the great hall in the center of town.

The snow was beginning to let up. Harold stopped several yards behind the sons at the edge of town. *I'm surprised they haven't noticed me following them,* he thought.

The sons headed to a small bazaar on one of the side streets. The first table was the town's butcher. Various cuts of meat hung from hooks above the table. Several legs were laid out on the blood-stained table. The boys touched different cuts of meat as they spoke to the butcher.

"Can you say E Coli?" Harold asked the ravens as he stood behind Gustav's sons.

"Shoo, you infernal pests," the butcher said to the ravens, waving his hands at them. Both birds pecked at one of the stacked legs and flew off with a small morsel.

"Holy crap, that's a horrible smell," Harold said, waving his hand in front of his nose. No reaction from anybody around him. He looked around with some confusion. "They can't hear me." He extended his arm to tap Ulfr on the shoulder, but his hand disappeared. "What the —?" he exclaimed, retracting his hand.

Henrik handed the butcher some coins and pointed at one of the hanging legs. The butcher pulled it off the hook and handed it to Henrik, who stuffed it into the leather bag slung over his shoulder. Henrik turned and began walking over to another table, then stopped in his tracks.

"What is it, brother?" he asked Ulfr. Ulfr was frozen in place, staring at something. Henrik followed his eyes and saw a beautiful young lady admiring some jewelry at another table. "Uh oh, someone's in love," Henrik said. He shrugged his shoulders and continued down the street without his brother.

The young maiden looked up from the table and was a little spellbound herself when she saw Ulfr. The two stared at each other and said nothing.

"Wow," Harold said when he got a good look at her. "You have great taste my friend, she's stunning." No reaction from Ulfr.

The young maiden was a bit shorter than Harold. She possessed an athletic beauty about her, long, lean, but strong as well. Her long blonde hair was braided in some places and flowed like a waterfall off her shoulders. Her emerald hazel eyes could light up any street in the dark of night.

Ulfr knew she was a noble's daughter by the immaculate dress she wore under her furs. Even though he heard his father's voice in the back of his head, "Stay away from the nobles' daughters," he couldn't take his eyes off of her.

Harold saw the connection between the two of them, and felt the electricity in the air. It made him think about Wendy; he missed her.

The young lady's friends giggled as they ushered her away. She looked back a few times at Ulfr as he watched her and her friends disappear into the crowd. A large hand slapped Ulfr on the shoulder. Ulfr snapped his head around.

Henrik was smiling ear to ear. "What's wrong?"

"I just watched my heart walk away," Ulfr replied.

"Brother, please. There are many women to chase here," Henrik said. "What makes her so special?"

"I see the man I want to be when I look at her," Ulfr said.

"Uh oh, you're smitten by her," Henrik said, pulling his brother down the street with him. "Let her go, brother. She's a noble and we're poor farmers. A barrel of mead will help you forget her. Come on," Henrik pulled his brother into the great hall.

Harold followed the two brothers into the hall. Henrik looked for their father when they entered and saw him speaking with the Earl by his chair. Gustav looked towards the entrance after the Earl pointed at the brothers. He smiled and waved his boys over to meet the leader of their region.

"My lord, these are my sons, Ulfr and Henrik," Gustav said proudly.

"My word, Gustav. You grow them big at your place," the Earl said with a hearty laugh.

Both sons knelt on one knee in front of the Earl. "My lord," they both said.

"Oh, get up, please. I was once a farmer like your father," the Earl replied with some humility. The boys rose back up to their feet and faced the Earl. "I just got lucky and killed the right man." The whole hall erupted in laughter. He looked at Gustav. "Gustav, you and your sons are my guests. Feast and drink as much mead as you can hold."

"Thank you, my lord," Gustav replied with a head bow. He gestured to the boys to walk over to the empty table towards the back of the hall.

The men sat down, Harold remained standing behind them, taking everything in. He admired the fine craftsmanship done on the hall. The woodcarving alone was breathtaking to him.

Food and horns of mead were swiftly placed in front of the weary travelers. They devoured the food, which was still warm from the fire.

After their bellies were full, Ulfr asked, "Father, why are we here?" Before Gustav could answer him, the Earl stood up and pounded the ground with his spear three times. A hush came over the hall.

"My brothers, my family and I welcome you to our home." The Earl's voice bellowed out over the crowd. The Earl's wife and daughter appeared and stood next to the noble.

"Hey," Harold said, pointing at the front of the hall.

Ulfr's jaw dropped open and his eyes lit up. The Earl's daughter was the young maiden he had been mesmerized with at the bazaar. Henrik tapped his father on the shoulder and then pointed at Ulfr.

"Uh oh," Gustav whispered. "I had that same look when I first saw your mother."

The Earl continued. "We will meet the Earl of the North Valley on the field of battle tomorrow." He held up his horn. "Some of us will be feasting in Valhalla tomorrow!"

The room exploded into cheers. Mead was spilled everywhere as the drunk vikings broke out into song. Gustav and Henrik stood up and joined in the singing while Ulfr simply stood and stared at the young lady. The Earl and his family toasted the hall and sang along. His daughter looked out into the crowd and instantly noticed Ulfr looking at her. She coyly smiled and toasted her horn at him. He blushed but somehow managed to smile and toast her back. At the same time, they joined in with the others as they sang the old songs about life, love and the gods.

Harold rolled over and opened his eyes when he heard the ravens cawing at him. "This is becoming a pattern, guys," he said. He sat up and looked around the great hall. "Where is everybody?" He stood up and stretched.

Both ravens took off and flew out of the hall. Harold walked to the large door and followed them outside. Some of the merchants were selling their goods as children played in the open square. Then it hit Harold; only women, children and elderly were here. "Where are all of the warriors from last night?" he mumbled. He looked up and saw the ravens flying north, over the dense forest.

He ran out of town and into the woods. After about a quarter of a mile, he felt a sharp pain in his side. "I need to do more cardio," he gasped between breaths. He continued on his way, walking at a brisk pace down the narrow path towards the opening on the other side of the forest. He came out onto a small hill overlooking the battlefield.

The ravens landed and stood on top of the hill, next to Harold. He saw two formidable armies facing one another in the hazy morning mist. On one side were the men and able women from the great hall, the Earl's army, and on the other side, the Earl of the North Valley's army.

The ravens silently watched the events unfold. Harold scanned the Earl's army to see if he could find Ulfr, Henrik and Gustav. "There they are," he said when he saw Ulfr amongst the warriors. Ulfr stood out because he was several inches taller than everybody on the battlefield and he wasn't wearing a helmet — his head was too big.

Now that's how you lead, Harold thought when he saw the Earl standing on the front lines with his fighters.

"Fine day for a fight," the Earl said.

"Every day is a good day to fight, my lord," Gustav replied.

"Indeed," the Earl said with a hearty laugh. "Your boys look ready."

"They are, my lord. We will fight to the death for you."

"Good, then we all will be drinking mead and feasting with the gods in Valhalla tonight!" the Earl yelled. His warriors cheered and struck their shields with swords and axes. The Earl leaned over towards Gustav and his sons. "Which one of you is the oldest?"

"I am, my lord," Ulfr replied.

"Bring me a victory today and I'll give you my daughter's hand in marriage, Ulfr." Ulfr was speechless in his surprise. "Your father has served me well over the years and I owe him a great deal for it. Do we have a deal?"

Ulfr was stunned and didn't mutter a word. Henrik laughed when he saw Ulfr and said, "I think you have a deal, my lord."

"Come on, boy, let's go tell her," the Earl said, grabbing Ulfr's arm.

"All the way back to town, my lord?" Ulfr asked.

"No, son, she's here with the other shield maidens." The two of them walked fifty yards over to the other side of the field. Ulfr saw a group of women readying their shields and swords for battle. "Frida!" the Earl yelled.

One of the women looked back. "Yes, Father?"

Joe Gregory

The young damsel from the bazaar now looked like a seasoned warrior. Her hair was tightly braided and pulled back to stay out of her face during battle. A mixture of dried up blood, from the morning sacrifice, and blue paint covered half of her face. Even with the hardened appearance, her beauty still shined through.

"Frida, this is Ulfr, Gustav's oldest son," the Earl said.

"My lady," Ulfr said, bowing his head.

"You two are to be wed after our victory here today."

"As you wish, Father," Frida said with an agreeing smile. She tried to contain her excitement, her attraction to Ulfr was just as intense as his was towards her.

"It's settled then," the Earl said. "Come on, son, let's get this fight over with. I'm thirsty." The Earl began walking back to the front lines.

"The men of the North Valley do terrible things to the women of their defeated foes," Ulfr said with a serious tone.

"Don't worry, I won't let them hurt you," Frida responded with a sly grin.

The other shield maidens giggled. Ulfr smiled and headed back to the front. Every few yards, Ulfr turned around to look back at Frida. Each time, he saw her standing in the same spot, looking at him.

Ulfr joined the Earl, his father and brother in the front.

"Well, what do you think, son?" the Earl asked.

"She's beautiful, my lord," Ulfr said.

"Well, clear your head, it's time to fight. Shield wall!" the Earl yelled.

The warriors on the front line brought their shields in front of them, chest high, and crouched down. The warriors behind them brought their shields over and rested them on top of the first row of shields, covering their heads.

Gustav yelled, "No mercy!" The warriors cheered.

"Hey," Harold said to the ravens. "That's my catch phrase." The birds sat silent. Harold saw a tiny figure standing on the hill, about a hundred yards away. "What's that little girl doing here?" he wondered aloud.

She was very small in stature, about three feet tall, with pale-white skin, lighter than snow. Her hair was long, white and pulled back into a ponytail.

The ravens saw her and relentlessly squawked at her. She calmly peered at them with her blood red eyes. Harold was a little shaken. *No iris, no pupils, just blood,* Harold thought. She showed no emotion when she brought her index finger over her lips, gesturing for the birds to be quiet. The ravens ignored her and continued.

Harold's attention was brought back to the battlefield when he heard the Earl rally his troops. "Let's send these sons of whores to Valhalla for an early supper! Forward!"

Both armies began advancing towards one another. Their chants and footsteps echoed across the valley. The pace quickened as they got closer to each other, eventually meeting in the middle of the battlefield. It sounded like two large ships ramming into each other.

The battle was at an impasse as both sides dug in to fortify their shield walls. Several lines behind Ulfr, some of the men moaned and fell to the ground. "Archers!" somebody cried out. The archers of the opposing army were picking off the Earl's men one by one from behind the wall.

Suddenly, Gustav fell to the ground, clutching his shoulder. An arrow was buried deep into his right shoulder. Without hesitation, Ulfr reached down, picked his father up and carried him away from the shield wall. He reached the women that were tending to the wounded on the back lines and carefully placed his father at their feet.

Gustav grabbed Ulfr's arm. "We have to get behind their wall and take out the archers." Ulfr agreed and nodded to his father.

"We'll take care of him," one of the nurses said.

Ulfr began marching towards the wall. He looked to see if Frida was okay. He marveled at her and her shield maidens. They handled themselves with brutal efficiency, cutting and slicing through men with catlike reflexes. They used the opposing foes' brute strength against them by being quicker and attacking them from different angles. They would side-step their enemy's deathblow and slice their back or belly open as they ran past them.

Frida smiled when she saw Ulfr checking to see if she was okay. She was doing the same with him.

She gave him a nod, letting him know everything was good. He nodded back and continued to the front line.

"Henrik!" Ulfr yelled. Henrik turned around. "Shield!" Ulfr said, motioning a going-over-the-line hand gesture.

Henrik nodded. He tapped several men on the shoulder. "Form a line, Ulfr is going over!"

The men lined up and crouched down, supporting their shields with their shoulders. They formed what looked like a staircase leading up to the shield wall. Ulfr ran towards them; the men readied themselves. He jumped up onto the first shield, then the second and so on. Each man pushed up as he stepped on them to give Ulfr some added height to clear the wall. Henrik pushed with all his might as Ulfr leapt off his shield and over the enemy's wall.

Ulfr came down hard onto a man's shoulder with his sword as he landed on the ground. The blade cut through muscle and bone. Blood spewed out in every direction and all over Ulfr's face and beard. He pulled an ax from his belt and began hacking and slashing. Some of the men on the shield wall turned to fight him, creating an opening for Henrik and the others to come through.

"Come on!" Henrik yelled, slashing his way through the line with his sword. The enemy wall fell apart and it was now an open battle.

The two brothers met and looked each other over for wounds.

"Good?" Ulfr asked.

"Good," Henrik answered.

"Frida," one of the shield maidens said, pointing at Ulfr. "He broke their wall." She was covered with the blood of her enemies but her smile still shined through when she saw her soon-to-be husband.

An arrow flew by Henrik's and struck the man behind him. Without saying a word, Ulfr picked a dead man up off the ground and used him as a shield. He charged at the archers. Henrik and the others were right behind him.

"By the gods, that is glorious," Frida whispered, watching Ulfr's charge on the archers.

Each arrow hit the man's lifeless body with a sickening thud as Ulfr moved quickly, getting closer and closer. Ulfr threw the man's body at one of the archers and followed it with his sword.

He stabbed one archer with his sword and swung his ax into another one's neck. Some of the other archers ran off, Henrik and the others in hot pursuit.

With the wall broken and the archers taken out, the battle was soon over. The Northern Earl's remaining fighters were cut down and sent to Odin's great hall.

Ulfr walked over to a fat, hairy man covered with furs. The man meekly held up a sword and pointed at Ulfr. Ulfr knocked it out of his hand and punched the man in the face.

The Northern Earl fell to the ground, covering his face with his hands. He pulled his hands away from his face and saw the blood dripping onto the ground. He looked at Ulfr. "How dare you. I am an Earl!"

"Not anymore," Ulfr said, grabbing the man's fur cloak and dragging him through the blood, ice and snow. The men cheered as he approached his Earl. He stopped in front of the Earl and released his grip on the cloak. "Your prize, my lord."

"Thank you, Ulfr."

The Northern Earl wiped the mud from his eyes. "At least let me die with honor so I may join my warriors in Odin's hall."

The Earl motioned for one of his men to give the Northern Earl a sword. One of his guards threw a sword onto the ground, landing it next to the Northern Earl. He gripped the handle and firmly held the sword in his right hand.

"I am ready," bowing his head, exposing his neck.

The Earl raised his sword up high over his head. "Farewell, old friend," he said. He forcefully brought the blade down onto the Northern Earl's neck, severing his head from his body. The headless body fell to ground as the warriors cheered.

"He's perfect," the little girl whispered. She turned and took a few steps back down the hill.

Harold was uneasy after witnessing the battle. *It's nothing like the movies,* he thought. He saw the mysterious little girl take three steps down the hill and disappear into thin air. "Where did she go?" he asked the ravens, but didn't get an answer.

The Earl reached down and picked up the severed head of his adversary by the hair. He held it up to for his army to see. "Tonight, we feast!" Frida came over and stood next to Ulfr and her father. The Earl grinned at them. "We also have a wedding to plan."

The newly betrothed smiled at each other as the Earl and his men began heading back to town. Frida looked up at her future husband and patted him on the chest. "See, I didn't let them hurt you." Ulfr laughed as she walked away to join her shield maidens.

Henrik and Gustav joined Ulfr. Without taking his eyes off of Frida, Ulfr asked, "Are you okay, Father?"

"It's just a scratch, I'm fine," Gustav replied.

Henrik looked at Ulfr, then at Frida and then back at Ulfr. "You're a fool, brother. There are so many women to be had."

"I just want one," Ulfr said.

Gustav wrapped his arms around his sons' shoulders. "I'm proud to call you my sons. You both fought well today."

"Thank you, Father," both men said.

Gustav began slowly walking away. "Come on, let's go get drunk."

Chapter 6

With each passing day, the weather grew colder and colder. The weeks flew by as the two families negotiated the dowry and terms of the wedding. Harold missed his life back home, Beatrice, he even missed Chad. But the thing that ate away at him was not seeing Wendy. He'd finally found the girl of his dreams and being away from home for so long had probably ruined his chances with her.

He sat at one of the long tables as the village prepared the great hall for the ceremony. The ravens quietly stood on the table in front of him. They knew he was feeling down. One of the birds walked over and rubbed its head on Harold's arm to comfort him.

Harold smiled and petted his feathered friend. "Thanks, buddy." The other bird hopped over and did the same on his other arm. Harold looked over at it. "I guess you want some petting too, right?" He petted his other companion as the villagers finished the final preparations.

The Earl entered the hall and inspected the room. "Well done," he said.

"Thank you, my lord," one of the villagers responded.

"Gather the others and let's begin the festivities!" the Earl bellowed.

Within minutes, the hall was filled with townspeople. In fact, the crowd spilled out into the main square in front of the hall. The Earl stood next to the pagan priestess at the front of the hall. Harold had positioned himself at the front of the hall, just to the side of the Earl. He had a raven on each shoulder.

Ulfr came in from the side and stood in front of the Earl and the priestess. A few seconds later, Frida did the same and stood on Ulfr's right side.

Ulfr leaned over and whispered, "You look beautiful."

Frida replied with a smile, "You clean up nice yourself."

They held hands as the priestess began the ceremony. After saying several passages, she looked over at Gustav. He nodded and handed Ulfr the family's heirloom, a large iron sword. Ulfr took it from his father and handed it to Frida.

"From this day forward, you are a member of our family," Ulfr said.

Frida accepted the sword and then handed it to one of her attendants. Then, the Earl handed her their family sword to give to Ulfr.

"From this day forward, you are a member of our family and are under my father's protection."

Ulfr accepted the sword and handed it to Henrik. The priestess held both of her hands out so that each father could place a ring in her palm. Then, she handed Ulfr a ring.

"Ulfr, place this on Frida's finger and repeat after me." Ulfr took the ring from her palm and gently slid it onto Frida's finger.

"Now say your vows."

"I, Ulfr, take you, Frida, as my one true love. I will laugh with you, cry with you and honor you for the rest of my days. My life and my heart are yours to keep, forever."

Harold's eyes teared up. He wiped them with his hand. He saw the ravens staring at him. "Allergies," he said.

The priestess handed Frida the other ring to give to Ulfr. She slid it onto his massive finger and repeated the vows.

"Join hands," the priestess said, wrapping an embroidered belt around Ulfr and Frida's hands. "You entered as two and will leave here as one. Let no man or beast come between you." She reached over to a bucket on the floor and pulled the blood-soaked brush out of it. Both, Ulfr and Frida closed their eyes as the priestess shook the brush at them, droplets of blood landing on their faces. "May the gods bless this union and you live a long and happy life!"

"Skol!" the Earl yelled, holding his goblet up to toast the newlyweds.

"Skol!" the entire hall responded, doing the same. The servants began bringing the feast and mead for each table.

Several hours later, the festivities were still in full swing when a voice cried out from the back of the hall. "The king is here!"

A hush came over the reception. Three figures appeared at the door, their furs covered with snow. The crowd parted down the middle, creating a path directly to the front of the hall.

King Harald pulled his hood back, revealing his long dark hair and beard. His two guards did the same. On their way towards the front of the hall, the villagers bowed their heads, saying "Your Grace" as he walked by.

The Earl stood up with open arms to greet his old friend. The king smiled and threw out his arms as well.

"My apologies, Gunther, for being late. The paths are a little tricky around this time."

"Not a problem, Your Grace. I'm delighted you showed up."

"I wouldn't have missed it for anything, old friend," the king said, hugging his loyal nobleman. He noticed the awkward silence in the hall because of his arrival. "Please, continue with the festivities," he said, grabbing a cup off the table. He held it up to the crowd. "Skol!" he toasted and took a drink.

"Skol!" his subjects replied. The musicians began playing their instruments again and the villagers continued eating and drinking.

"You've grown up so fast, Frida. I remember being here when you were born." The king hugged the new bride.

"It's good to see you again, Your Grace," Frida said, hugging the king.

"Is this the lucky man?" Harald asked, looking at Ulfr.

"This is my new husband, Ulfr, Your Grace."

"It's a pleasure to meet you, Your Grace," Ulfr said, bowing his head.

"The pleasure is mine, Ulfr. I've heard great stories about you and your prowess on the battlefield."

"Thank you, Your Grace," Ulfr said, humbly.

"Let's enjoy this night with food and drink. We'll talk in the next day or two about what we're going to do after the ice thaws and what our plans are for heading west to England," the king said, sitting down to a plate of food.

The reception consisted of eating, drinking, and passing out, then repeating the same for three days. After a day of recuperation, a meeting was held. Attending the meeting was the king, the Earl, his advisors, the village elders, Gustav, Henrik, Ulfr and Frida. Harold sat quietly in the back of the room.

The king stood up to address the room. "My friends, I am raising an army to sail west, to England, and crush the Saxons. They have been a thorn in our side and it's time to remind them again that Thor's hammer is mighty and unforgiving."

"Yes," Henrik said, pounding his fist on the table. Others cheered.

The king wanted to rally his troops. He looked at Ulfr. "What say you, Ulfr? Will you go with me to kill many Christians?"

"Gladly, Your Grace," Ulfr responded, rising up to his feet.

"Yes! And you Henrik, there are many riches to be had there. Will you take them with me?"

"Without question, Your Grace!" Henrik said, jumping up off the bench.

"And you, Frida. You and your shield maidens are highly respected warriors. Are they ready for a fight?"

"Yes they are, Your Grace. As am I," Frida said, holding her sword up.

"Good!" King Harald yelled. "Enjoy this time. Eat, drink and be with your loved ones. I will go back and summon my army. When the ice thaws, I will return with one hundred ships to pick you up. Then, we will sail to England to crush those sons of whores! Skol!"

"Skol!"

Chapter 7

Frida leapt out of bed when she heard the village horns. It was the signal that boats were approaching. Ulfr moaned and turned over onto his other side.

"Ulfr, my love, get up. The king is coming," she said, trying to dress as quickly as possible.

Ulfr picked his head up. Frida was still naked, trying to pick the best outfit to receive the king. Ulfr stealthily climbed out of the bed. "It'll take some time for all those ships to dock, my love," he said, grabbing her around the waist.

"Ulfr, no, we don't have time for this," she said with a smirk.

Ulfr picked Frida up and carried her back to bed. "We have time for one more, beautiful."

Frida giggled and passionately kissed Ulfr.

Harold walked out from behind a tree. "What was that?" he asked the ravens perched on a branch above him. The ravens squawked and took off towards the harbor. "Wait up!" Harold said, shaking the dew from his lily. He retied his trousers and jogged after the birds.

He came out of the woods and stepped onto the stone-covered beach. "Whoa," Harold said, looking out at one hundred Viking ships coming into port. He recognized King Harald on the first ship approaching the dock.

The Earl and his subjects were waiting on the docks to welcome the king. Harold saw Ulfr and Frida running from their house towards the dock. They ran up and stopped next to the Earl, both of them breathing heavy.

"My apologies, my lord, but your daughter takes forever to get ready," Ulfr said with a mischievous grin.

"What?" Frida said. "Father, we were late because of this giant oaf," she said, smacking Ulfr hard on his bottom.

"I'll help with the ropes, my lord," Ulfr said, running down the dock. Frida couldn't contain her smile.

The Earl shook his head. "Ah, young love." Frida hugged her father and kissed him on the cheek. "I'm glad to see you happy, my dear."

"I couldn't be happier, Father. Ulfr is my everything and I am his."

The Earl kissed his daughter on the forehead. "Let's go greet the king," he said, wrapping his big arm around her. The two of them strolled down the dock.

"How was your trip, Your Grace?" Ulfr asked, throwing the rope onto the boat.

"Thanks to the gods, Ulfr, it went well," King Harald replied.

Joe Gregory

The dock man secured the king's boat. The other boats of the fleet anchored in the harbor and began loading into rowboats to come ashore.

The king jumped onto the dock and hugged Ulfr. "Good to see you again, Ulfr."

Ulfr bowed his head, "Your Grace."

The king turned and saw the Earl approaching. "Gunther, you old bear!"

"Your Grace," the two large men laughed as they hugged one another. "Come, eat and drink with us."

The king faced his men coming in on the rowboats. "Men, eat and drink your fill tonight. We sail for England tomorrow." The army cheered.

The king and the Earl led the way to the great hall with the village inhabitants and the king's men followed them. Ulfr and Frida slowly walked behind the crowd. All of them marched past Harold without noticing him. Some even walked through him. However, Ulfr paused and stopped right next to him.

"What's wrong, my love?" Frida asked.

"I don't know. I felt something here," Ulfr said, pointing to where Harold was standing. "Something not of this world but also familiar at the same time."

The ravens squawked from the tree branch. Frida glanced at them and then back at Ulfr. "The ravens think you had too much to drink last night," she said with a laugh.

Ulfr laughed as well. "Perhaps you're right, beautiful." He wrapped his arm around his wife and they continued heading for the hall. Occasionally, he would look back to see if something was there.

Harold looked at the ravens. "Does he know I'm here?" The birds squawked. "Thanks, you're a lot of help."

Chapter 8

"Land, Your Grace. Land!" one of the crew yelled, pointing at the English coastline.

"Good," King Harald declared, slapping Ulfr's shoulder with his mighty hand. The sea breeze blew his hair away from his face, revealing many facial scars from battles of love and war.

"What are the Saxons like, Your Grace?" Ulfr implored.

"Their knights and soldiers fight with ferocity, but their leaders are fat and soft. They only take for themselves and don't value their men," the king replied. "They also hide behind their Christ-God and have forsaken the old ways. It makes them weak and ripe for the taking." Ulfr nodded, taking everything in. The king winked at him. "They're no match for us." Ulfr smiled. "Make for land!" the king commanded.

The crew adjusted the sails and signaled the other boats. The Norse armada set course for the coastline.

As they approached, Harold saw a small figure watching them from the hills overlooking the beach. "No way," he mumbled. "It's the little girl from the battlefield." The ravens began to caw incessantly.

Her pale skin and white hair almost blended in with the surroundings. However, there was no overlooking her blood-red eyes peering out across the water. A cold shiver ran down Harold's spine. The crows were still voicing their disapproval of the little girl. For a split second, Harold turned to look at the birds and then back at the coastline. She was gone.

"Where did she go?" The ravens also went silent.

The fleet was now several hundred yards from the beach. "Anchor here!" the king ordered. "We'll go in with the small boats. I don't want those bastards burning our way home."

The crew laughed and agreed. They began lowering the rowboats onto the water's surface. *Intelligent move,* Harold thought. *The boats are out of range of Saxon archers. They're not mindless beasts like some scholars would have you believe.*

The first boats to reach the beachhead were full of men and women prepared for war. Each warrior was armed with a sword, several axes and multiple hidden knives. The king also made sure his warriors wore their heavy chain mail under their leather and furs. The Britons swung heavy broadswords. That kind of blade did a lot of damage when it made contact.

Once they scouted the area, the all clear was given for the supply boats to come in and set up camp.

King Harald gathered a small raiding party consisting of Ulfr, Henrik, Frida and ten of his men. Like a wide-eyed kid in a toy store, he looked at them. "Let's have some fun." They quietly marched up the embankment and disappeared over the dune.

A lone rider approached the castle at breakneck speed. "A rider approaching," one of the sentries shouted.

The watch commander recognized the scout. "Open the gate," he commanded.

The gates slowly opened as the rider kept up his pace. He barreled through the opening and yanked the reins when he entered the main courtyard. One of the soldiers grabbed the reins while the scout dismounted. A knight strode out from the stable to meet him.

Trying to catch his breath, the scout struggled with his words. "I have urgent news for the king."

"What is it?" the knight inquired.

"The Sea Wolves are here, my lord."

"Sea Wolves?" the soldier holding the reins asked.

The knight had a look of concern on his face. "Norsemen," he replied in disbelief. He quickly gathered himself and looked at the scout. "This way," he said, marching towards the entrance. The scout hastily followed him inside.

The scout followed the knight through a maze of long hallways, finally coming to the large wooden door of the main hall. Two members of the king's guard stood on each side of the door. They were in full armor and armed with a shield and spear in each hand. Both had large side swords sheathed on their sides and several daggers in their belts.

"We have urgent news for the king," the knight said. The guards didn't flinch as knight and scout walked through the door and into the main hall.

The hall where the king held court was cold and dimly lit. Although there were torches on each of the massive stone pillars and also on the walls, the shadows of the room still danced across the stone. The dreary English weather didn't allow the sunshine to come in through the windows.

The two men marched towards the front where the throne was positioned. On the side, the king was enjoying a hearty lunch. He stared at the young male cup bearer with a promiscuous gaze. The English king was an equal opportunity lover, enjoying both men and women.

"News from the coast, my king," the knight said.

The king reached over and grabbed the cup bearer's butt. "Oh, my Liege, you frisky devil," the young man said.

"I'll see you later," the king cooed. He brought his cup up to his lips and took a swig of wine.

Growing impatient, the knight said, "Norsemen, my king."

The king spit his wine out onto the floor. "What?" he barked.

"The Norsemen have arrived and are making camp by the ocean, Your Grace," the knight said.

The king rose from the table and walked over to the two men. He glared at the scout. "Tell me, boy. Out with it."

"They've already raided a couple of towns, Your Grace," the scout sputtered. "They're giants, my king, and fight like mad bears."

"I'll summon our forces, Your Grace, and we will go deal with the heathens," the knight confidently declared.

"Wait," the king said, before the men walked off. "How many ships did you see?" he asked, addressing the scout.

"Around two hundred, Your Grace."

"Oh my god," the king whispered. He looked at the two men. "We're going to need many more men to fight them." He began to pace back and forth, formulating a course of action. He stopped and glanced at the scout. "Stay on them and report everything back to me, directly."

"Yes, Your Grace," the scout replied, bowing his head.

The king walked over and stood in front of the knight. "Send riders to my brothers' kingdoms. We'll need men, horses and supplies. It will take time to raise an army so make haste and be quick about it."

"My Liege," the knight responded.

Both men bowed, turned around and marched out of the hall.

"God save us," the king mumbled, standing alone in his great hall.

Chapter 9

All through the spring and early summer months, the Norsemen raped, pillaged and plundered their way across England, unopposed. All of the men, and some of the women, enjoyed the spoils of the flesh except for Ulfr and Frida. They only wanted each other, a rarity in their culture.

Harold marveled at how ferocious Ulfr was on the battlefield, cutting down the enemy with ease, and how gentle and kind he was with Frida.

Ulfr and Frida were lying by a small stream just outside of camp. Harold sat several yards away from them, enjoying the rare sunlight himself. Ulfr's big burly arms were wrapped around Frida, holding her tightly.

Frida raised her head from Ulfr's chest and looked at him. Her smile gave her away.

"What is it, my love?" Ulfr said, opening his eyes.

"I haven't bled in two moons, dear," Frida replied.

"What?" Ulfr sat up in disbelief.

"I'm with child, my love. You're going to be a father," Frida uttered with tears of joy in her eyes.

Ulfr's eyes welled up with tears as well. "I'm going to be a father?"

"Yes."

"That's wonderful. I love you so much," Ulfr said, hugging Frida and kissing her on the cheek.

"That's awesome," Harold mumbled, wiping a tear from his own cheek.

Harold watched from afar how their love for each other grew every day, and became very attached to the couple. He was a bit envious and wondered if something like that would have developed with Wendy. But he had been gone from home for so long, he thought he would never know that kind of eternal love.

"Ulfr, Frida!" Henrik yelled from the edge of camp. Harold, Ulfr and Frida stood up and looked over at Henrik. "The scouts are back with news!" He waved for them to join the war council.

Ulfr acknowledged Henrik with a wave. He turned to Frida and rubbed her belly. "This changes everything, you can no longer fight with us. You must protect the baby."

Frida touched the side of Ulfr's face. "I know, my love."

"You two are my everything, my eternal," Ulfr declared, passionately kissing Frida.

"And you are ours," Frida replied.

"Damn allergies," Harold mumbled, rubbing his eyes as he followed them back to camp.

The king and his leaders were listening to the scout's report when Harold, Ulfr and Frida approached the large table.

"Good work," the king said, patting the scout on the shoulder. "Get this man some food and ale," he ordered. One of the servants led the scout over to the food tent.

Ulfr and Frida took their place next to Henrik at the table. The king glanced around and did a head count. "Good, everybody's here." He rolled out a large parchment onto the table and weighed down each corner with a stone.

Ulfr leaned in towards Henrik. "What's going on?"

"I think we're going to get the fight we've been looking for, brother," Henrik answered.

The Norse King hovered over the map and pointed at it. "The good King of Wessex has summoned his brothers' armies, numbering in the thousands." Some of the leaders began stroking their long beards, analyzing the numbers and calculating a plan of attack. "Everything up to now has been easy. Now, we earn our way into Valhalla."

"Yes, finally," one of the commanders said.

"They have many foot soldiers which isn't a problem," King Harald stated. "My concern is their heavy cavalry. Hundreds of well-armed knights will be upon us tomorrow." The king glanced over to one of his generals. "But we're ready for that, right?"

"Yes, Your Grace. Our long spears, along with the trenches we dug, should even the odds greatly."

"Good." The king looked at Ulfr and Henrik. "Ulfr, Henrik, you and your men will engage the main force head on."

"Gladly, Your Grace," the brothers replied.

"Frida, you and your shield maidens will flank them from the right."

Ulfr quickly interrupted the king. "My apologies, my king, but Frida won't be joining us on the field tomorrow," Ulfr said, rubbing Frida's tummy.

"I am with child, Your Grace," Frida added sheepishly.

"Congratulations, brother," Henrik said, hugging Ulfr.

The king came around the table and wrapped his arms around Ulfr and Frida. "What wonderful news," he said with a huge smile on his face. "He'll be a fierce warrior like his mother and father."

"Who said it'll be a boy, Your Grace?" Frida asked with a sly grin.

The king and the council let out a hearty laugh. He hugged the two again. "Well done." The king made his way back to the head of the table. "With that news, Frida, who will be in command of your maidens?"

"Helga, Your Grace," Frida responded.

"Good." The king was pleased. "She's a good warrior and will do well." He motioned to one of the young servants. "Go fetch Helga."

"Right away, Your Grace," the young man said. He ran over to the maidens side of camp and retrieved her.

Once she joined the others on the council, the king continued with his battle plans. A while later, he finished the presentation and stood tall. "Agreed?" he asked his generals.

"Agreed," they responded.

"Eat and drink well tonight. We go to war at first light." Each person departed for their tents to gather their things and prepare for battle.

Nightfall came within a few hours as the smell of cooked venison filled the air around camp. The servants had set up the large tables in the center of camp. Barrels of ale were tapped, and plates of carved venison were placed on the tables along with vegetables.

Miles away, the King of Wessex was enjoying his evening meal. His three brothers, along with a few knights, were discussing the strategy for the next day's battle. They were interrupted when the king's guard entered the tent.

"What is it?" the king barked.

"The scout has returned, my Liege."

The king wiped his mouth on his sleeve. "Send him in." The guard exited the tent and came back in with the scout in tow. The scout bowed. "Well, what news do you bring?"

"My king, I found the Norsemen camp," the scout humbly stated.

The king's eyes widened. "Really, do tell," he said with a devilish grin.

Chapter 10

Frida heard something rustling in the tent. She turned over and saw Ulfr collecting his weapons for the day's battle. It was still dark out, just before daybreak.

"Are you wearing the heavy chain mail for their broadswords?" she asked, sitting up in bed.

"I'm sorry, my love. I didn't mean to wake you," Ulfr replied, walking over to the bed. He quietly sat next to her. "I am," he said, pounding his chest twice.

Frida stroked his long hair and beard. "I know we are warriors, but please be careful. Come back to me." She leaned in and kissed Ulfr.

After the kiss, Ulfr rested his forehead on Frida's. "I promise, my love." He rubbed her belly. "I'll be back for both of you." Frida kept a brave face and nodded. The sounds of footsteps and steel grew louder with each second around the camp. Ulfr stood up. "I better go. I love you," he said, walking out of the tent.

Frida's eyes teared up. "I love you," she responded. Then she whispered, "Come back."

Harold was up before the others and waited for them on the hill. He also knew the routine for going to battle well. After many months of not shaving or having his hair cut, he looked like a Norseman.

It was business-like. The men assembled at the edge of camp and marched towards the battlefield. There was no yelling, no bravado, they were quietly efficient. They were deadly shadows in the early morning darkness. Not that anybody could see or hear him, but Harold walked alongside of them without making a sound as well.

The heathens covered the terrain quickly and positioned themselves on the battlefield before the first rays of sunlight broke through the darkness. Harold walked over and took his place on a hill, overlooking the battlefield.

The first rays of sunlight broke out from their nocturnal prison and raced across the sky. Some of the beams reflected off the armor of the knights and soldiers standing across the field from the Norsemen. As the men began to get riled up and cheer, Ulfr remained silent. He surveyed the Christian army and took mental notes.

Five hundred mounted knights, he thought. *One thousand foot soldiers with two hundred archers behind them.* He saw the king, his brothers and their guards on the hill behind the main army. *We have a little over a thousand men and women, should be a fair fight.*

King Harald and a few of his generals were the only Norsemen on horseback. He rode in front of his army, waving his sword in the air to rally the troops. The heathens responded by cheering and banging their weapons on their shields. Once the ruckus calmed down, King Harald sat calmly on his steed and stared at the English. His most trusted soldier rode up next to him.

"Let's say hello," King Harald said, not taking his eyes off of the English army.

"Archers!" his general yelled. Two row of archers stepped forward. "Nock!" The archers readied their arrows on their bows. "Draw!" Each archer pulled back with all his might. "Loose!" The archers released their arrows.

The arrows whistled as they cut through the morning sky, like an ominous flock of birds carrying death with them.

One of the English archers leaned over and whispered to his mate, "Should we be worried?"

"Nah, they're too far out of range. It's all for show."

The arrows finally reached their apex and began their descent towards the English army. Within seconds, several of the soldiers and archers moaned before falling lifeless onto the ground.

"Shields!" one of the knights yelled as death came from above.

The archer that said the Norsemen were out of range was struck in the neck. He fell to the ground, clutching his throat in an attempt to stop the bleeding. It didn't work; he was dead in a matter of seconds.

While chaos ensued in the English ranks, King Harald took advantage of the distraction. "To Valhalla!" he yelled as he charged forward. His horsemen and soldiers followed, running at full speed towards the Christians.

"Archers!" one of the English knights yelled. What was left of the archers gathered themselves. "Nock!" They readied their arrows. "Draw!" They pulled back and aimed for the approaching horde. Before the knight could yell, "Loose!" the archers began falling and screaming. Frida's shield maidens were picking them off en masse from the tall grass on their right flank.

Suddenly, before the English commander could give the command to retaliate, he felt two arrows strike him in the back. The arrowheads had pierced his armor. One penetrated his right lung. The other went into his spine. He struggled to breathe as he used the last ounce of his strength to turn around. Frida's shield maidens were attacking them from the left flank as well. The mighty knight fell from his horse and took his final gasps of air before dying.

"My God," one of the English king's brothers said. "These savages don't fight with honor."

"No they don't. They fight to win," the king replied. "Send in the cavalry," he commanded.

"Send in the cavalry!" his top knight repeated. One of the foot soldiers signaled the knights by waving the cavalry banner.

"With me!" one of the knights declared, repeatedly kicking his horse on the sides. The animal took off at full stride. The other knights quickly followed their leader.

After the archers and some of the foot soldiers were taken out, the shield maidens began firing on the charging knights. Knight after knight fell from their horse and met their doom. The maidens ran out of arrows. But in the process, they took out several hundreds of the knights.

"That'll even the odds a bit," Helga said. She unsheathed her sword and charged towards the English foot soldiers. The rest of the shield maidens followed her lead.

"Are those women?" one of the soldiers asked. Before he got his answer, the maidens were already cutting through the first line of soldiers.

"Shield wall!" Ulfr shouted. Even though the maidens did an excellent job of decreasing the number of mounted knights, a hundred still remained and they were charging towards the Norsemen.

The front line stopped, knelt down and placed their shields in front of them. The second line came in behind them and placed their shields on top of the front line. The third line came in and held their shields over their heads. Ulfr, Henrik, the spearmen and the other foot soldiers stood behind the wall.

The men cheered as King Harald and his generals charged towards the approaching knights. It was ten Viking horsemen against a hundred mounted knights.

"Open!" Ulfr shouted. He looked at Henrik. "We have to protect the king." The men opened the shield wall to let Ulfr and Henrik run out to help the king. The men cheered again as the two brothers sprinted towards their king.

"My God, he's not stopping," the commanding English knight whispered.

One of the vikings threw a spear, striking the commanding knight in the chest. He flew off of his horse and hit the ground hard. The last thing he saw were hooves striking the ground before running over the top of him.

King Harald stood up in his saddle, holding his sword straight out in front of him. When his horse violently collided with the first line of knights, the impact threw him forward. The knight he hit directly, along with both horses, died instantly. The king sailed through the air like a spear and impaled a knight in the second line.

King Harald and the knight fell off the back of the knight's animal as it ran away. His horsemen did the same, killing man and beast with each collision. The king jumped back up to his feet and pulled an ax from his belt with each hand. With extreme prejudice, King Harald began chopping at anything resembling an Englishman. Only a few knights stayed back to battle the king and his generals.

In a full sprint, Henrik brought his spear up to his shoulder, took aim at the approaching knight and heaved it with all his might. The spear sailed past Ulfr and struck the knight in the face thirty yards ahead of them. By now, the lines were disorganized, there was space to maneuver around the riders.

In one swift motion, Henrik pulled the spear from the knight's chest as he ran by, without breaking stride. A knight was holding his sword high overhead, barreling down on Ulfr. Ulfr pulled back with both hands on his sword and chopped off the front legs of the horse. The poor beast fell face first into the dirt. The knight was thrown off and was struggling to regain his composure to continue fighting. Ulfr ran over and stabbed him in the chest. His body quivered as blood oozed from his mouth.

Another maimed horse fell by Ulfr. Henrik drove his spear deep into the animal's chest and then slit its riders throat. Ulfr, along with Henrik, King Harald and his generals, continued their onslaught on the knights of the Realm.

Seventy or so knights continued their charge towards the shield wall. "Brace yourselves!" the commander yelled. The sound of the horses impacting the Norsemen's shields rang out across the battlefield. The sickening thud was soon followed up by the screams and cries of horses and men. The brave knights were systematically butchered by the Viking horde.

After the shield maidens had made quick work of the foot soldiers, they joined King Harald and the others in decimating the remaining knights. When the smoke cleared, King Harald looked around at his countrymen and women. They were all covered from head to toe with blood and mud. They were exhausted, some wounded, but they were alive and had defeated the enemy.

The king held his hands out, widened his eyes and stuck his tongue out at the English king and his brothers. "Ahhh!" he yelled in victory.

"Your Grace," one of the king's guard said. "Your safety is of the utmost importance. We must get you back to the castle."

The English king saw a column of smoke in the distance, rising above the forest. "That should keep them busy for a while," he mumbled.

"What's that, brother?"

The king looked over at his brother. "I, too, play to win."

Ulfr noticed the English king looking past them at the forest. "What is he looking at?" he murmured, turning towards the forest. He saw the smoke rising into the sky. *Frida,* he thought. "My king, look!"

King Harald saw what caught Ulfr's attention. "The camp. Quick, Ulfr and Henrik, go!" The two brothers ran over and each grabbed a stray horse. They took off towards the forest.

"Come, brothers," the English king said, turning his horse around. "Let us make haste." The small group retreated down the hill and headed back to the keep.

Harold jumped up and saw the smoke. He took off running towards the camp as well. He blinked and was suddenly back on the edge of camp. *How did I get here so quickly,* he wondered.

The camp was in pandemonium, women and children were running and screaming. Others lied dead on the ground. While the Viking warriors had been engaged with the armies of England, the English king had dispatched a group of assassins to destroy the camp and its inhabitants.

Harold saw a tiny little figure in the forest overlooking the camp. *Holy crap, that's the little girl from Norway. What is she doing here?* There was no mistaking her pale-white skin and blood red eyes. She silently watched the carnage, taking pleasure in the killing of innocents.

Something caught her attention and she peered over at the path. Harold heard the hooves pounding the ground as Ulfr rode in. He leapt off his horse and saw a group of Englishmen surrounding the last person standing. It was

Frida. Three men already laid dead at her feet. She had a cut on her arm and was obviously battle weary. Even pregnant, she was still an efficient killing machine.

The loss of blood from the cut momentarily dulled her senses and she stumbled. One of the English swordsmen took advantage and lunged in with his blade, impaling Frida in the stomach. Her eyes went wide as she dropped her sword and gripped the assassin's blade with both hands. She stared into his eyes as the blood oozed from her mouth and down her chin. He pulled his blade out and she fell to her knees, trying to stop the bleeding from her stomach.

Another man lunged in and drove his sword through her back. "Noo!!!" Ulfr shouted.

As he charged at them like a crazed beast, Frida fell face first onto the ground and stopped breathing. Henrik arrived and saw his brother charging the group of Englishmen. Then he saw Frida lying dead on the ground.

"Bastards!" he yelled as he dismounted and followed his brother.

While in full stride, Ulfr pulled two axes from his belt and launched them at the men. They found their targets. Both men were knocked off their feet with an ax in their chest.

"Yes, yes," the pale little girl mumbled.

Ulfr then threw his sword, hitting another man in the shoulder. He dropped his weapon and fell to the ground. Ulfr pulled the axes from the other mens' chests as he ran by. Henrik had an ax in one hand and a sword in the other as he ran into another group of assassins coming towards them.

Ulfr stopped by the wounded man and chopped him in the face with his ax, killing him instantly. He pulled his sword out of the man's shoulder and continued his onslaught.

Harold cried seeing Frida die the way she did. Sadness quickly turned to rage and he wanted blood himself. He tried to run and help, but his feet wouldn't move. He summoned all of his strength but couldn't lift his foot a millimeter off the ground. He heard the little girl giggling. He looked over and she was wagging her finger at him.

"You're not allowed to help, Harold," she said. Her voice sent shivers down Harold's spine. It was ancient and evil. *How does she know my name?*

Ulfr beheaded the last man near him. His rage quickly turned to a painful sorrow when he knelt down next to his soulmate. He sobbed as he turned Frida over and held her in his arms. He gently rubbed her bloody stomach.

"I'm sorry I didn't get here sooner, my love," he mumbled.

Henrik ran his sword through the last man standing. He made sure they were all dead before kneeling a few feet from Ulfr.

He tried to console his brother. "Frida and your son are in Valhalla now, brother. They will feast with the gods tonight."

Ulfr just wept and nodded in agreement.

Henrik rose to his feet and patted Ulfr on the shoulder. He walked away so Ulfr could have some time to himself. Suddenly, an arrow raced past Henrik's head and into Ulfr's chest. Ulfr was in such despair that he didn't react to the arrow striking him in the chest.

Henrik quickly ran over to a bow lying on the ground to return fire. By the time he set the arrow, aimed and released it into the tree line, two more arrows had already sunk into Ulfr's stomach and throat. Henrik killed the hidden archer with one shot, but it was too late.

Ulfr fell over onto the ground, still holding Frida. His will to live was gone, he wanted to join his wife and son in Valhalla.

Henrik began to run towards his brother but froze in place. Everything went silent, the wind, the sounds of war, everything. Harold felt the earth stop. Time was at a standstill.

The little girl walked away from the tree line and into the camp. She enjoyed the bodies lying about as she walked by them. When she reached Ulfr, she stopped and stood over him. He was still alive, barely. The little girl grabbed his arm and turned him over onto his back with ease. She looked down into his glazed-over eyes.

Harold was quite a distance away from them but could hear her whisper to him. "You'll be with your beloved again, Ulfr. If you help me, I'll make sure that happens."

The sky overhead became cloudy and dark. Harold looked up when he heard the thundering hooves from above.

"Valkyries," Ulfr muttered, blood gushing from his throat wound.

The little girl became enraged when she saw the choosers of the slain emerging from the heavens to take the dead to the AllFather. She hissed when they landed to collect the dead, exposing her razor-sharp fangs and long, forked tongue.

"Step aside," Hildr commanded, climbing off her heavenly steed. She was the leader of the Valkyries and had served Odin for millennia. "We're taking them to the Great Hall," Hildr said, drawing her sword.

"No," the little girl hissed. "They're mine." She drove her clenched fist into the ground, causing a massive explosion and a blinding ray of light.

Harold was knocked unconscious, Hildr was thrown several feet away, landing on her back. She jumped back up to fight, but Ulfr, Frida and the little girl were gone.

Chapter 11

Harold moaned as the ground beneath him moved back and forth. The familiar rhythm of the motion made him a bit nauseous. In addition to the slight concussion from being knocked unconscious. He struggled to open his eyes when he heard waves crashing around him. He panicked when he saw the wolf's snout a few inches above his face.

"Ahh," he screamed, trying to crawl away from the beast. A split second later he recognized his rescuer. "Oh, it's you," he said, rubbing his head. He realized that he was at sea on the unmanned Viking boat again.

Seeing that Harold was shaken by the ordeal but unharmed, the wolf calmly walked back up to the bow of the boat and sat down. Harold collected himself and rose carefully to his feet. He looked around and saw nothing but open ocean all around them. He had a lot of questions.

Harold slowly made his way towards the wolf and stood a few feet behind it. "Who was that little girl or thing?"

The wolf didn't take its eyes off the ocean ahead. But, Harold saw its ear bend so he knew it heard him.

"Why am I here?" Still no response. Frustrated but thankful, Harold decided to rest some more. "For what it's worth, thank you for saving me," he said.

The wolf turned his head, looked at Harold and nodded. Harold nodded back and gave a half-hearted wave as well. He quietly walked to the middle of the boat and lied down on the deck.

A few hours later, the wolf nudged Harold with its paw. Harold woke up and asked, "What's going on?" The wolf motioned for him to follow it to the bow.

Harold stood up and stretched. Then, he followed the wolf to the front. He scanned the horizon and saw land. *That coastline looks familiar,* he thought. *I've been here before.* He quickly looked around. *This is the English Channel, that's France. Where are all the buildings?*

The boat made its way to shore and came to a stop when the hull breached the sand. The wolf jumped out of the boat and onto the beach. After it shook off the sea mist from its fur, it motioned for Harold to disembark and follow it.

"Okay," Harold said, leaping off the boat.

He followed the wolf to the edge of the beach, where the grass met the sand. Harold heard a lot of commotion coming from the field on the other side of the field. He saw hundreds of tents scattered in front of a large castle. It was a military encampment. Some of the men were practicing their sword skills against one another. Others were tending to the horses, while others were eating.

"I wish I knew what they were saying," Harold said, trying to guess the language the men were speaking. The wolf leaned over and licked

Harold's ear. "I guess we're buddies now?" he said, rubbing the saliva from his ear. He froze when he realized he understood what the men were saying now. "How did you do that?"

The wolf began walking back to the boat. Harold started to follow it, but it stopped and shook its head. "I'm not going with you?" he asked. "What am I supposed to do?" The wolf pointed at the army with its snout. Harold turned to look at the camp and then back at the wolf, but it was gone.

Before he could start yelling profanities, Harold noticed a lone figure, standing next to his horse a quarter mile down the beach from him. His gut told him that he had to walk over there. As he got closer to the man, Harold noticed it was a knight.

His armor was battle-worn with several dents and dried up blood stains on it. However, the wolf's head on the chest plate shined through. Harold looked over and saw the knight's helmet on the horse's saddle. It was a wolf head. *I bet he looks like a crazed werewolf in battle,* Harold thought.

The dark knight's horse became restless when something emerged from the ocean. "Easy," the knight said to his trusted companion. Then he stared at the phantom approaching him with his ice-like blue eyes. Years of war and conflict had made this man into a fine-tuned warrior.

"No way," Harold mumbled when he recognized the pale-white girl walking towards them.

She calmly stood in front of the knight. "You know what you have to do," she said. The knight held his hand out. The little girl placed two rings onto the man's callused palm. He bowed his head.

As he placed his foot in the stirrup and mounted his horse, the little girl looked at Harold. He had never felt fear like that before as she looked into his soul with her blood-red eyes. Without saying a word, she turned around and walked back into the cold, unforgiving sea.

The knight's horse trotted off the beach and headed towards the castle. Harold shook off the uneasy feeling and followed the knight and his horse. The rank and file soldiers cheered as the knight rode through camp, heading towards the castle gate.

"Popular dude," Harold mumbled.

One of the watchmen on top of the fortress wall saw the knight approaching. He immediately recognized the rider by his signature armor.

"It's Lambert, open the gates!" he shouted.

The two guards by the door lifted the heavy wooden beam with all their might and pushed it to the side. Then, each guard grabbed a door handle and pulled the large wooden doors open.

A few seconds later, Lambert's horse stormed into the inner courtyard. A stable quickly ran over to hold the reins as Lambert dismounted.

"It's good to see you again, my lord. Prince Godfrey is expecting you," the young man said.

"Are the others here?" Lambert asked, pulling his gloves off.

"Yes, my lord."

Lambert petted his horse's neck. "Be nice to Phillip," he whispered into the animal's ear. The horse nodded. Lambert then pulled out several silver coins from his belt. "Thank you, Phillip." He placed the coins into the young man's hand.

"Thank you, my lord. I'll take good care of him for you."

Lambert marched past the door guards and went inside the castle. Harold was close behind. He soon heard voices as they made their way through the maze of hallways.

They finally entered into the room where Godfrey held court. The dimly lit room was large and cavernous, flanked on each side by massive, round pillars, one every ten feet. The room went silent when he walked in. Harold was in awe at the number of knights in the room. He gazed up to the front and saw three Frankish princes sitting on beautifully ornate chairs.

Godfrey stood up and looked over the crowd and saw Lambert. "Good of you to join us, Lambert."

"My apologies for being late, my lord," Lambert humbly replied.

"Nonsense," Godfrey answered. "I'm just glad you decided to join us on our quest."

Lambert bowed and took his place among the other knights. The knight standing next to him leaned over and whispered. "What made you change your mind about coming with us to Jerusalem?"

Without taking his eyes off of the princes, he replied, "My destiny takes me there."

Jerusalem? Harold thought. It took a few seconds for him to digest everything. "Holy shit," he mumbled. "This is the first crusade."

"Knights!" Godfrey bellowed. "His holiness, the Pope, and the Council of Clermont have ordered us to take back the holy land in the name of our Lord!" The knights cheered. "Let's prepare for the long journey and drive those heathens out of Jerusalem!"

Another knight greeted Lambert after the speech. "I'm glad you are coming with us to do the Lord's work."

Lambert coldly stared into the knight's eyes. "I'm not doing it for your god or any other gods. I'm going there to do what I do best, kill men."

Before the knight could reply, Prince Godfrey approached the two men. Lambert and the other knight bowed.

"Excuse us, I need to speak with my commander," Godfrey said to the knight.

"My lord," the knight responded and walked away.

Godfrey placed his hand on Lambert's shoulder. "Ready the troops, old friend."

"My lord," Lambert responded.

Chapter 12

The princes' most trusted knights and personal bodyguards were readying their horses in the castle's inner courtyard. Moving an army comprised of thousands of knights and soldiers to the Holy Land would be a long and arduous task.

Harold stood next to Lambert as he prepared. The knight next to them leaned over towards Lambert. "An army is already on the way to Jerusalem," he said. "I heard they are led by some priest called Peter the Hermit."

Lambert stoically replied, "A bunch of undisciplined fanatics. They are no army."

Godfrey and his brothers stepped out onto the elevated platform overlooking the courtyard. Each knight, squire and servant bowed their heads with respect for the princes. Soon after, they were joined on the platform by the archbishop of the region, a personal confidant of the pope.

Godfrey addressed the group first. "The archbishop will now give us his blessing."

The archbishop raised his arms in the air. "Please, kneel." All present, including the royals, knelt, except for Lambert. He stood up tall and defiant. He caught the archbishop's attention. The cleric glared at him with a disapproving scowl. "Kneel!" Lambert didn't flinch.

One of the other clergy pointed at him. "He must kneel!"

Some of the archbishop's entourage began marching towards Lambert. The dark knight calmly placed his hand on his sword and waited for them. Godfrey suddenly jumped up and intercepted the holy men.

"He's my top commander. I will vouch for this man," Godfrey declared.

Another priest spoke. "It's sacrilege to defy the church. We will make the heretic kneel before God!" he demanded.

Godfrey placed his hand on the priest's chest and looked into his eyes. "That'll be the last thing you will do on this earth. Because if he doesn't cut you down, I will," he said with an authoritative tone.

All of Godfrey's knights rose to their feet and drew their swords. Harold marveled at the amount of respect each knight and also the prince had for Lambert.

"There will be no need for violence. Please, let us continue," the archbishop pleaded.

His priests stepped back to their place behind the archbishop. Godfrey gave the signal for his knights to stand down and he walked back over to his brothers. His knights sheathed their swords and went down on one knee.

"Lord, bless these brave men on their pilgrimage and protect them from your enemies. Also, give them the strength to enforce your justice and vanquish the heathens and unfaithful. In your name we pray, amen."

All except Lambert responded, "Amen."

"May God be with you," the archbishop concluded, giving the men the sign of the cross.

As the clergy meandered back into the safety of the castle, Godfrey and his brothers made their way off the platform and over to their men.

Lambert bowed when Godfrey approached him. "My apologies, my lord. I didn't mean to embarrass you in front of the church," he humbly stated.

"Not to worry, my friend," Godfrey reassured him. "We have given generously to the church in the past. They can overlook some of our indiscretions," Godfrey added with a wink. "Not only are you my best advisor and most trusted knight, you are also my dear friend, Lambert."

"Thank you, my lord."

"Plus, I was saving those poor bastards from you," Godfrey said with a hearty laugh. Lambert actually cracked a smile. "Enough with the formalities, let's be on our way."

"I'll ready the men, my lord."

After Godfrey lifted himself up onto his horse, his knights followed suit. Lambert rode out before anybody and ordered his captains to ready the troops for departure.

The princes led the procession out of the castle. All of the knights and men outside the walls bowed as they rode by. One by one, each army fell in behind them and marched. After making sure the men were in place, Lambert rode up towards the front and took his place along with the other knights.

Godfrey looked back and waved for Lambert to ride forward and join him.

"My lord?" Lambert inquired.

"My brothers bore me. Will you ride and chat with me?" Godfrey asked.

"Of course, my lord," Lambert agreed.

The two men discussed strategy and warfare for a few miles. Soon, the subject bored Godfrey as well.

"Still no woman in your life?" he asked Lambert.

"No, my lord," Lambert answered.

"It's just us, you can drop the 'my lord' part," Godfrey said.

Lambert smiled. "Okay, my—," Godfrey pointed at him. "Okay."

"I can give you one of mine," Godfrey said. "Or do you prefer men?"

"No. I had a wife once, but she died many years ago," Lambert replied solemnly.

"I'm sorry for your loss," Godfrey said, trying to console his long-time friend. "But you have to move on sometime. Why not with a beautiful young maiden?"

"Thank you, but my heart and soul belong to one woman," Lambert replied.

"Fair enough, I won't push you to do anything you don't want to," Godfrey said.

"Thank you," Lambert answered.

"That just means there will be more for me," Godfrey bellowed with a laugh. Lambert actually laughed as well.

The crusaders rode and marched all day. Just before nightfall, the army stopped and made camp.

"I'm going to retire for a bit before supper," Godfrey said, climbing down from his horse.

"My lord," Lambert acknowledged. He dismounted and gave the reins over to a squire. "I'm going to get cleaned up myself," he said to another knight.

That sounds like a great idea, Harold thought, following Lambert to the nearby lake.

While Lambert was painstakingly taking his armor off, Harold looked into the water and saw his reflection. "Damn," he mumbled, running his hand down his long beard. He heard Lambert walking into the water. He chuckled when he saw how white Lambert was from the neck down. "Knight's tan."

The next morning, a scout rode into camp and stopped by Godfrey's tent. "Yes?" Godfrey said, exiting from his tent already dressed in full armor.

The scout jumped from his steed and bowed. "My lord, the village ahead has been sacked. Everybody is dead."

"What?" Godfrey inquired. "By whom?"

"I don't know, my lord, but I found several of these on the ground," the scout replied, holding up a small iron cross.

Lambert came over, the scout placed it in his hand. He studied it. "This is the same cross our priests wear, my lord," he said, handing it to Godfrey.

"Let's go take a look," Godfrey said to Lambert. He pointed at two of his guards. "You and you, with me." The guards snapped to attention and ran over to ready their horses.

While the squire prepared Godfrey's horse, Lambert ran over and saddled up his horse. The four men took off in the early morning light while the others broke camp.

Harold took two steps and was suddenly at the edge of the war-torn village. Godfrey, Lambert and the two guards rode in and stopped in the middle of the village. Lambert was the first to dismount and draw his sword. He scanned the perimeter for any movement. When he felt it was safe, he gave the all clear for Godfrey and the guards to climb off their horses.

Embers were still smoldering on some of the burned out dwellings. Smoke billowed from the windows. Corpses were strewn all over the ground with missing limbs and heads. One of the bodies had on priest's robes. Lambert carefully walked closer and pushed the body over with his foot. It was one of Peter the Hermit's priests.

"Murders," Godfrey said, standing by Lambert. He pointed at some of the villagers' bodies. "These people are jews. Those bastards are killing non-Christians on the march to Jerusalem."

"These people were innocent," Lambert said, gritting his teeth.

"We'll deal with those zealots when we catch up to them," Godfrey proclaimed.

A noise came from one of the huts several feet away. Instinctively, Lambert stepped in front of Godfrey before his guards had time to react. When the guards came over, Lambert silently walked into the hut. He saw something move under a blanket in the corner. He moved like a cat towards it, not making a sound. The predator was stalking his prey. With his sword at the ready, he ripped the blanket off but momentarily froze when he saw a frightened little boy cowering on the floor.

"Easy boy, I won't hurt you," he said. "Come with me, you're safe now." He picked the toddler up and pulled him tight against his chest. He still held his sword ready in case of any other surprises. "My lord," he said, walking out and setting the child down in front of Godfrey.

"What happened here?" Godfrey asked, kneeling in front of the boy.

At first the child was reluctant to speak but relaxed when he saw that they meant him no harm. "Men came and hurt people," the child said, pointing at the dead priest.

"Your mother and father?" Godfrey asked. The child pointed at two bodies by the hut. The men sighed and bowed their heads.

Harold saw a woman bolt out from the nearby trees. She frantically ran towards the men. Lambert spun around and took a defensive stance in front of Godfrey. The guards did the same.

"Raymond!" she screamed.

"Stop right there or I'll cut you down," Lambert ordered. She paused, tears running down her cheeks.

"You know this child?" Godfrey inquired.

"Yes, my lord. He is my sister's son," she responded. She looked back at the bodies of her sister and brother-in-law and gasped. "Dear lord," she mumbled in between tears.

The boy ran over and hugged his aunt. Godfrey followed. "Take him to safety," he said, handing her a bag of silver. "Make sure he has a good life."

"Thank you, my lord. I will," she said, picking the child up. She placed the bag of coins in her pocket as the child wrapped his arms around her neck. Godfrey motioned to one of his guards. "Make sure they get home safely."

"My lord," the guard answered. He helped the woman and child get on his horse. He climbed up and sat on the saddle behind them. With a sharp kick to the horse's ribs, they trotted off down the road.

Chapter 13

A little over a year after they left the northern
Frankish kingdoms, the Christian armies of
Godfrey and his brothers arrived at the ancient
city of Antioch. It was founded by one of
Alexander the Great's generals in the fourth
century BC. It was also the center of Christianity
during the Roman Empire. The Byzantines and
Arabs had fought over the city for centuries.

"The halfway point between Constantinople and Jerusalem," Godfrey said, studying the large walls of the great city. "The perfect place for future crusades to resupply and gather reinforcements before heading to the holy city."

"Indeed, my lord," Lambert said, counting the guard towers showing above the wall.

The armies of Robert and Bohemond had captured the Iron Bridge on the previous day and were now camped on the southern wall. Godfrey and his army positioned themselves on the northwest walls.

The knights lined up and dismounted for the blessing before the siege began. All of the men knelt down on one knee except for Lambert. He stood tall and continued searching for any weaknesses on the city walls. The priest stopped and glared at Lambert. Lambert ignored him.

"Proceed, Father," Godfrey ordered.

The priest began sprinkling holy water on the men as he walked down the line. "On this, the twenty-first day of October, in the year of our Lord 1097." The men did the sign of the cross when the water hit them. "May Prince Godfrey and his Christian warriors strike hard and true in your name, oh

Lord. In the name of our father, the son and the holy spirit. Amen."

"Amen," the men repeated.

Lambert wiped the water from his brow. The men stood back up and readied themselves for battle.

Godfrey looked over at Lambert. "Let's get started. Shall we?"

"My lord," Lambert replied with a bow. "Send the signal!" he shouted at an archer.

The archer lit his arrow on fire and pulled back with all his might. After he released the arrow, it cut through the air with surgical precision.

"My lord, the signal!" one of Robert's soldiers yelled.

"Ready the catapults!" Robert shouted to his troops.

Lambert did the same from his location. The men loaded enormous boulders into the bucket, showered them in oil and lit them on fire. He gave the signal to each group leader. They, in turn, ordered their men to launch the projectiles.

"Loose!"

One by one, the ropes were released and the giant arms unleashed hell upon Antioch. Unfortunately, the boulders had little effect on its mighty walls.

Harold sat behind the catapults, mesmerized at the constant barrage. He'd read about sieges in books but now, he was actually witnessing one firsthand. He was amazed at how well the walls were holding up. Godfrey and Lambert also watched as the stones turned into rubble on impact.

"Well, this may take some time," Godfrey stated in a sardonic tone.

That was an understatement, the siege continued into the winter months. During breaks in the action, the crusaders sent out foraging parties to find food, wood, and the other necessities. At the same time, the Turks would send out small groups of armed men to ambush the Christians, mostly at night.

In late December, Godfrey fell ill. Lambert briefed him several times a day, every day, to keep him up to speed on the battle.

"Why the face, Lambert?" Godfrey asked between coughs. "Is it that bad?"

"It's pretty grim, my lord," Lambert said.

"Go on," Godfrey urged.

"The famine is decreasing our numbers dramatically. Many of the men are dying from starvation, about one in seven men. The ones that are still living are starting to desert. Peter the Hermit and his group left camp during the night."

"Cowards," Godfrey mumbled.

"It's affecting the horses as well, my lord. We only have seven hundred remaining."

"Any good news, old friend?"

"Actually, there is," Lambert said. "Robert and Bohemond took twenty thousand men on a foraging party and intercepted Duqaq in Albara. They were en route to relieve Antioch."

"What happened?" Godfrey asked.

"Both sides took heavy casualties but Duqaq was defeated and his supplies were brought here."

"Was he captured?" Godfrey inquired.

"No, my lord. He's probably on his way back to Damascus as we speak," Lambert replied.

"With his tail between his legs!" Godfrey shouted with a hearty laugh.

Lambert laughed, then continued. "I'll believe this when I see it, but it's said that the English will arrive here in early Spring to help, my lord."

Godfrey heard the tone of Lambert's voice change. "What's wrong, Lambert?"

"I apologize, my lord. I don't like the English."

"Neither do I, but we need them to accomplish our mission," Godfrey added.

"Agreed," Lambert said, rising to his feet. "You need to rest, my lord. I'll be back this evening."

"Thank you, Lambert," Godfrey said before falling back to sleep.

The siege continued into the summer of 1098. Godfrey regained his health and once again fought alongside his troops.

"My lord." A rider approached Godfrey and Lambert. "We've breached the main gate."

"Finally," Godfrey said with relief. He turned to his men. "Let's take the city!" The men cheered and followed his charge.

Harold blinked and found himself standing by the side of the massive gate, just inside the city. Godfrey and Lambert were at the forefront, hacking and slashing at adversaries with their swords. The crusaders went street by street, slaughtering the Turks along the way.

Hours later, the crusaders controlled most of the city. As Godfrey and the other princes met to establish control and rule of the city, Lambert and his knights set to patrolling the streets. Lambert suddenly heard a woman screaming from one of the side alleys. He jumped off his horse and ran down the alleyway. His knights were close behind.

They came to an opening where he saw five English soldiers attempting to rape a woman. Her small child was standing just feet away witnessing the impending horror. Two of the soldiers were holding the woman down while one other soldier was lying on top of her, trying to undo his trousers. The last two were standing watch.

"Fuck off, nothing to see here," one of the watchmen said.

Lambert didn't say a word as he marched towards them. The two watchmen drew their swords and took a defensive posture. Like a cat, Lambert ducked under the swing of the first soldier and sliced his belly open as he went by. As he stood up, he ran his sword through the other soldier's throat. Lambert withdrew his blade and the man's lifeless body fell to the ground.

The soldier on the woman was trying to pull his trousers back up and draw his knife from his belt, but Lambert knocked him unconscious by striking him on the head with the hilt of his sword. The last two soldiers released the woman but were quickly disarmed by Lambert's knights. Lambert reached down and lifted the unconscious soldier off of the woman.

She kicked and screamed. Lambert calmly looked into her eyes. "We're not going to hurt you. You're safe now." He looked over at the child and then back at the woman. "Take your little one and find a safe place to hide."

She quickly jumped to her feet and ran over and hugged the child. They both took one last look at the knights and ran away.

"When King Edgar hears about this, you lot will be drawn and quartered," one of the soldiers growled at Lambert.

Lambert walked over and punched the man square on the nose, breaking it. The man cried out as he bled profusely. The other soldier remained silent.

Lambert pointed at the quiet soldier. "Take your friends and leave now before I kill the rest of you."

The soldier bent down to pick up his unconscious comrade. He looked up at the man with the broken nose. "Get down here and help me."

The man reached down with one hand, his other hand trying to staunch the bleeding. They managed to get their friend upright and draped his shoulders over theirs. The trio stumbled off.

"This isn't over!" the man with the broken nose yelled. "I'll see you again!"

One of the Frankish knights leaned over. "That's a scary threat, Lambert. I hope you can sleep tonight." The other knights laughed. Lambert said nothing.

A Frankish horseman approached. "My lord. Prince Godfrey is requesting that you return to the garrison at once."

"On my way," Lambert said, walking over and inserting his foot into the stirrup.

A few minutes later, Lambert and his knights entered the garrison. Godfrey stood over a large wooden table, holding a parchment in his hand.

Lambert walked over. "You needed to see me, my lord?"

Godfrey handed the letter to Lambert without speaking. Lambert saw that is was a scouting report.

A large muslim army, under the command of Kerbogha, has left Mosul and is heading towards Antioch. They have joined up with Ridwan's army and also Duqaq's army.

"My lord, once we fortify the city—," Lambert started to say.

"Look at the date," Godfrey interrupted.

Lambert saw that the letter was several weeks old. He calculated the distance and speed of the armies. "That means they'll be here within the week."

"Our scouts spotted them a day's ride from here, old friend," Godfrey said, staring at the window. "Prepare the troops, we'll meet them outside the city."

"My lord," Lambert replied and marched out of the war room.

"I pray for a miracle," Godfrey mumbled.

Harold followed Lambert as he briefed his knights and gave the orders to ready the armies.

Two days later, Godfrey, Lambert and the rest of the army were finishing the last minute preparations for the ensuing battle. A commotion broke out when news of the Holy Lance traveled amongst the troops.

"My lord," one of the knights said to Godfrey. "One of the priests found the Holy Lance."

"Where?" Godfrey asked.

"In the city, my lord."

"Fools," Lambert scowled.

"Perhaps, but if we can use it to rally the troops, it might lead us to victory," Godfrey mumbled to Lambert.

Harold chuckled. He remembered reading about this very thing in a history book. Many of the crusaders had been suffering from starvation and were prone to hallucinations.

"We will be victorious today, my lord. God sent one of his angels down to punish the Turks."

"See?" Godfrey whispered, smirking at Lambert. Lambert smiled and nodded in agreement.

Harold remembered that the "angel" was actually a meteorite entering the atmosphere and it appeared to fly over the Turkish army.

A hush of silence came over the army as Raymond of Aguilers rode through the ranks, carrying the Holy Lance. Everyone except for Lambert and Harold, bowed their head and did the sign of the cross as the lance went by.

After it went by, Godfrey climbed up on his horse. "That's our cue."

Joe Gregory

"Mount up!" Lambert commanded. The knights climbed up and sat at the ready. "Onward to battle!"

The knights fell in behind Raymond, and the foot soldiers behind the riders.

Kerbogha and his massive army watched the Christians emerge from the ancient city. The crusaders were divided into six regiments as they approached the battlefield.

"We should strike now," one of Kerbogha's commanders said.

"No," Kerbogha responded.

"We need to hit the front lines hard and fast."

"I said, no!" Kerbogha barked. "It will weaken and divide our forces."

The commander stewed with anger as he and Kerbogha continued watching the crusaders exit the city. Minutes later, Kerbogha showed signs of nervousness. The crusader army was much larger than he anticipated.

"Use the archers to lure them out and separate their ranks," Kerbogha ordered. The commander rode off and gave the order.

156

The Turkish horse archers rode forward and unleashed a barrage of arrows on the crusader foot soldiers. Meanwhile, the main Turkish army attempted to lure the Christians into unsteady land by faking a small retreat.

"Predictable," Lambert said.

"You were right, old friend," Godfrey admitted.

"Hold your positions!" Lambert ordered. "Do not follow them!" He pointed to a banner man to give Bohemond the signal to attack their flank. The banner man furiously waved his flag.

On the other side of the battlefield, Bohemond saw the signal and ordered the charge. "With me!" He and his regiment attacked the Turkish flank, cutting their soldiers down with ease.

Kerbogha sat in silence, shocked at the size and ferocity of the crusader army.

His commander rode back over to him. "Fool, we should have attacked them as they left the city," he snarled. He rode off and ordered his troops to retreat from the battle.

The other Emirs followed suit and began pulling their armies away from the battle. The final straw was when Duqaq took his forces and left. Most of the men were under his command. The remainder of the Turkish army was defeated and in disarray. Kerbogha retreated a broken man.

The crusaders cheered and rejoiced in their victory before making their way back into Antioch.

Lambert dismounted his horse and handed the reins over to the squire. As he pulled one of his gloves off, something out of the corner of his eye caught his attention. Harold saw it too.

The little pale-white girl with red eyes strolled through the main gate and entered the city. A shiver ran down Harold's spine when she glanced over at them. Lambert stood unfazed.

She stopped when she reached the main square of the city. "Go, my children," she said, opening up her robe. Suddenly, thousands of rats poured from her robe and ran out into the city streets.

"Oh my god," Harold whispered. "She's releasing the plague on the city."

"My lord," Lambert said, marching towards Godfrey. "We must make for Jerusalem immediately." His voice held a sense of urgency.

"Let the men enjoy and celebrate their victory for a few days, Lambert."

"I believe the city has been cursed, my lord. Death is here and we must leave at once," Lambert pleaded.

Godfrey had never seen Lambert show any kind of fear until now. "You have never steered me wrong, my friend," Godfrey said, placing his hand on Lambert's shoulder. "Give the order. We depart at once."

Chapter 14

What was meant to be a five-week journey to the Holy City slowly stretched into a year-long struggle. The crusaders left Europe with five thousand knights and thirty thousand foot soldiers. Now, because of war, famine and disease, their numbers had diminished to fifteen hundred knights and twelve thousand soldiers. Many of the crusaders wept with relief when they saw Jerusalem.

"Finally," Harold said, sitting down on a nearby rock. He pulled a knife from his belt and proceeded to cut his sweat-soaked beard.

It was the beginning of summer and the temperatures were increasing with each passing day.

While most of the Christians fell to their knees and prayed, Godfrey and Lambert remained on their horses. Both men were analyzing the surrounding area and creating a battle plan.

"Clever devils," Godfrey said. "They cleared all of the vegetation around the walls so their enemies would be exposed during an attack."

"Not to mention we'll have to find the materials for our siege weapons somewhere else," Lambert added.

The muslim Fatimids had conquered the city one year prior and taken it away from the Turks.

"Forage what we can, I'll confer with the others. We attack tomorrow," Godfrey said, before riding off.

"My lord," Lambert answered.

Overnight, they could only muster a couple of catapults and several fifty-foot ladders for the initial siege. At first light, the siege began. Godfrey wanted to test the city's defenses and only sent lesser knights and a few thousand foot soldiers. Reluctantly, Lambert promised to stay behind with Godfrey.

Many men and horses collapsed and died from thirst and hunger before reaching the walls. The ones that persevered were slaughtered. During the carnage, a scout approached Godfrey.

"My lord."

Godfrey shook his head and rubbed his eyes. "Yes," he said. "Any word from Antioch?"

"No relief will be coming from Antioch, my lord."

"It gets better and better," Godfrey growled. "Why not?"

"Thousands have died from the plague, my lord. Bohemond can't spare any men."

Godfrey's eyes went wide and he glanced at Lambert. *How did he know?* he wondered.

"But I also bear good news, my lord."

"Go on."

"The Genoese supply ships have arrived and are at the port of Jaffa, my lord."

"Ships?" Lambert inquired.

Godfrey and Lambert each knew what the other was thinking. "Go back and tell the captain that we'll be using his ships to build siege engines. And, if he gives you any trouble, tell him he'll have to answer to me."

"My lord," the scout answered. He turned his horse around and took off at breakneck speed back to the port.

Lambert felt a burning sensation in a hidden pocket underneath his armor. "I'll spread the word, my lord," he said, bowing to Godfrey and making a quick exit.

"Thank you, Lambert."

Harold followed Lambert as he took a quick detour behind a tent. The dark knight cautiously looked around and determined he was not being watched. Harold watched him dig under his armor and pull something out. When Lambert uncurled his fingers, two rings glowed in the palm of his hardened hand. The rings the pale little girl had given him on the beach.

"She's here," Lambert whispered.

Harold noticed that the expression on Lambert's face was one of both joy and pain. *Who's here?*

Lambert quickly placed the rings back in his hidden pocket and marched away.

It took a little over a month for the ships to be dismantled and transported to the camp, along with much-needed food, water and other supplies.

While the final preparations were being made, some of the lesser knights, Peter the Hermit and the other religious zealots, thought that their current plight was exactly like the city of Jericho. In order for them to breach the walls of the Holy City, they had to walk around it, barefoot, and their prayers would make the walls crumble to the ground.

Godfrey's army watched as they marched around the perimeter of Jerusalem.

"Fanatics," Godfrey said.

"Idiots," Lambert added. They both went back to their discussion of the battle plan. "In a couple days, my lord, we'll have five catapults, a battering ram and two fifty-foot siege towers."

"Good," Godfrey said. "We'll attack at night and use the cover of darkness to our advantage."

After the priest gave the blessing, the crusaders waited for darkness. In the dead of night, the catapults unleashed their fiery barrage on the great walls of the Holy City. While the explosions lit up the black sky, Godfrey and his troops began moving the siege tower towards the northwest wall, while another group began positioning the other tower on the southern wall.

The rocky, uneven surface created mayhem on the wooden wheels of the towers. Somehow, the other tower reached its position quickly and they began their assault. For two hours, Godfrey's men slogged their tower towards the northwest wall as they watched the other tower being pelted with oil and fiery arrows.

Men began jumping from the southern tower, trying to avoid a fiery death. Most broke a limb on impact and thus couldn't get out of range of the muslim arrows quickly. They were picked off one by one.

Suddenly, something raced by Lambert's head and hit the knight's chest sitting next to him. Then another one whistled by as it cut the night air, striking another knight in the throat.

"Arrows!" Lambert yelled. He quickly pushed Godfrey off his horse and fell to the ground himself. The arrow impaled the saddle Godfrey had just been sitting in. "Take cover behind the tower!" Lambert ordered.

The knights dismounted and ran over to join the foot soldiers behind the structure.

Godfrey got up and dusted himself off. "Thank you, Lambert," he said before the two ran over to the others.

"How can they see us?" a foot soldier asked. No one had an answer.

Lambert glared at the enflamed tower in the distance and then down at his armor. "Our armor," he stated matter-of-factly.

"What?" a knight asked.

"Our armor is giving off a reflection from the fire," Lambert answered, undoing the leather shoulder straps of his armor. "Take it off so they can't see us."

"But, we'll be vulnerable," another knight complained.

"It'll give us a fighting chance," Lambert replied.

Godfrey barked, "You heard the man, off!"

The knights began discarding their heavy armor. Lambert poured some water over himself and reached down and grabbed handfuls of dirt. He smeared the earth all over his face and head so he would blend into the night.

"Brilliant," Harold said, admiring Lambert's ingenuity. "This wasn't in the history books."

To make things better, the other tower finally collapsed and the flames started to dim.

"Archers," Lambert whispered. "Create a distraction and buy us some time. Take out as many of their archers as you can."

"Yes, my lord," the archer commander answered.

They cautiously stepped away from the tower and formed a line. The muslim archers were still randomly releasing their arrows into the dark, but had no idea they were about to be answered back tenfold.

The commander gave hand signals to his archers. The men drew their bows back and paused. He then gave the release signal.

"What's that sound?" a muslim archer asked. A split second later, an arrow impaled his eye. The archer fell forward and landed on the ground outside of the wall.

"Go," Lambert said, helping the others push the tower a few more feet towards the wall.

Panic set in amongst the muslim wall guards as the unseen arrows continued claiming their victims. A wall commander could see the tower now.

"Douse the tower with oil!" he commanded. "Set it ablaze!"

Lambert and the others started to climb the tower ladders as the muslim guards tipped the large pot of oil over. If they had any chance of succeeding, they had to reach the top before being burned alive, and go over the wall. The crusaders struggled with their grip and footing as the oil washed over them.

"Hurry!" Lambert shouted, climbing up the ladder.

A man above him lost his grip and fell past him. Lambert didn't have time to stop his fall or mourn the man. He had to reach the top so he could save the others. A few seconds later, Lambert reached the platform in front of the breaching bridge. He swiftly kicked the door, causing it to slam atop the wall.

With his sword in one hand and an ax in the other, he charged at the guards like a crazed beast. They were gripped with fear.

"Night demon!" one of the guards shouted before running away.

Before the others could react, Lambert was already on top of them. He cut down three of them before they could defend themselves.

Godfrey reached the platform and saw Lambert cutting down anything within his reach. "Come on!" he bellowed to his troops. "Help your brother!" He ran across the bridge and dove onto a guard.

"They've made it over the wall, my lord," a soldier said, notifying the battering ram commander.

"Good. Another hit and this gate will fall," the commander replied. True to his prediction, the battering ram impacted the door one last time. The large iron gates buckled and fell.

"For God and country!" one of the soldiers yelled, charging through the opening.

The rest of the troops armed themselves and ran to catch up with their comrade.

"Where are the guards?" another soldier asked.

"They must have retreated once the walls were breached," the commander answered.

Crusaders flooded the city streets and began indiscriminately killing all non-Christians. Men, women, children, it didn't matter.

From high above the city, on the wall, Lambert looked down in horror. He glared at Godfrey. "Is this the way of your God?" he asked in anger.

"No my friend, it is not," Godfrey replied with the same anger. He shouted to his brothers, "Combatants only, no innocents!" But his demand fell on deaf ears.

The lawlessness raged on for another week before order was restored. Lambert and his knights were quickly making enemies by denying the spoils of war for the other Christians. Even though he was a prolific killer of men, Lambert tried to live his life with some sense of honor.

It was decided by the dukes and princes that Godfrey would be named *Advocatus Sancti Sepulchri* or the Defender of the Holy Sepulchre. The council tried earlier to name him the King of Jerusalem, but Godfrey believed there was only one king worthy of that title, Jesus Christ.

The crowning ceremony was already underway. In the main courtyard, a long walkway started at the entrance and ended at the foot of Godfrey's throne. Christian knights in ceremonial armor were lined up and standing on both sides of the walkway, facing one another. A bishop and his court surrounded Godfrey's throne and watched as a priest slowly marched down the path.

Behind the the priest were two monks carrying a beautifully ornate box made of gold. They stopped at Godfrey's feet and placed the box gently on the ground. The bishop stepped down and opened the box. He pulled out a new, shiny crown and scepter.

Lambert stood towards the back and out of sight. He wasn't a fan of such pomp and circumstance. Harold was next to him.

The bishop stepped over and positioned himself behind Godfrey's throne. He handed the scepter to another clergyman and held the crown with both hands, over Godfrey's head. "In the year of our Lord, 1099, and by the power of the Catholic Church and God himself, I declare Godfrey *Advocatus Sancti Sepulchri,* Defender of the Holy Sepulchre and Guardian of Jerusalem," the bishop exclaimed.

Cheers erupted throughout the courtyard. Lambert clapped his hands with approval. He felt that Godfrey was a good and honorable man, and was the right man for the job. Harold also clapped and whistled.

Lambert flinched when he felt the burning sensation in his pocket again. Only this time, it was much more intense. Harold watched as Lambert pulled the two rings from his pocket. When Lambert opened his hand, the rings glowed brilliantly and gave off a humming sound.

Suddenly, they heard a woman's faint cry for help. Lambert instantly ran out of the courtyard and down the street. Harold was in fast pursuit. They momentarily paused and listened intently. *There it is again,* Harold thought.

The two men ran down the street, searching house to house to find the woman begging for help. The cries became louder, they were getting closer. Lambert rammed the door of the last house with his broad shoulder, shattering it to pieces.

Harold ran in behind him. The inside of the house was dark and dingy, dust floated on the rays of what little sunlight shined in. Lambert saw a body on the floor, against the wall. The young muslim woman was weaker now and could only let out a soft moan. He knelt down and gingerly turned her over on her back.

Lambert wept when he saw her mesmerizing hazel eyes. Harold's eyes began to water as well. The woman had obviously been beaten, raped and left for dead.

"I'm sorry I wasn't here to save you, my love," Lambert uttered. His tears fell upon her cheek.

My love? Harold thought.

The woman mustered up enough strength and whispered, "Behind you, my love."

Before Lambert could react, a dagger pierced the side of his neck and came out of his throat. Frantically, Lambert grabbed his throat to slow the bleeding but it was too late. The blade had cut through his esophagus and sliced his carotid artery. Blood spewed from his throat as he struggled to breathe.

"No!" Harold screamed, punching the assailant. His fist passed through the man's head. There was nothing he could do to stop it and he gasped in frustration.

The assassin stepped out of the shadows. "I told you I would see you again." The Englishman's crooked nose was a stark reminder of Lambert's justice in Antioch. "I was going to pay you back for this," he said, pointing to his nose. "No matter how long it took." He laughed when he walked out of the house.

Lambert only had a few seconds of life left in him. He pulled himself closer to the woman. They touched each other's faces and took their last breaths together.

Harold was speechless, tears ran down his face. He spun around when he felt the familiar cold shiver down his spine. The pale little girl with red eyes was standing in the doorway. He back-peddled and pressed his back against the wall.

She looked at him but only for a second. Then her attention turned towards Lambert and the muslim woman. She slowly walked in, almost floating across the room. Her long white hair was tightly pulled back, braids running down her back.

Once she reached the couple, she paused and just stared at them. Then, she reached down and took the rings from Lambert's cold grip. She held them in her hand and looked at Harold. He was frozen in fear. *What do I do?* kept running through his head. Without any emotion, the little girl floated towards the door. She exited the house and disappeared into the sunlight. A bright light engulfed the room, blinding Harold.

Chapter 15

Harold opened his eyes as the blinding light faded. Bewildered, he frantically looked around him and realized he was back on the boat. Once again, the large wolf was standing on the bow, staring at the horizon up ahead.

"Hey," Harold snarled in anger. "What the hell was that?" The wolf briefly turned and looked at Harold, but brought his gaze back to the waters ahead. "Why am I here?" Harold continued, marching towards the wolf.

Against his better judgement, Harold tapped the wolf's hind leg. "Hey, goddamn it, I asked you a question."

The wolf slightly turned his head and growled. Harold quickly came to his senses after he heard the warning. "Sorry," he said, taking a few steps back. "I'm confused, I don't understand any of this." He began walking back to the stern. "It's hard for me to watch people suffer and not be able to do anything about it."

The wolf knew Harold's heart was in the right place and that he was just frustrated.

Harold got his bearings and saw land on both sides of the ship. *We're on a river,* he thought. *I hope I get some answers by the end of this journey.*

The ride upriver was quiet and uneventful, with calm waters and a comfortable air temperature. It cooled off a bit when the early evening came, but it was still tolerable. After nightfall, Harold could see fires glowing in the distance on both sides of the river.

The next morning, Harold was rudely awakened when two airplanes flew over the vessel. He quickly jumped up. Unfazed, the wolf merely watched the planes continue up the river. Harold recognized the insignias. "Luftwaffe?" he asked, perplexed. "German planes?" he continued walking towards the bow.

The two planes gained altitude and veered right. They continued towards the center of the large city, dodging ground fire coming from hidden positions. Once they reached the center of town, both planes released bombs.

The target was a large burned-out building. Each bomb found its target and smashed the ruined building into a smoking pile of rubble. The boat's bow ran up the river bank, about a mile downriver of the city, and came to a stop. The wolf jumped off of the boat and landed on the riverbank. It motioned to Harold to follow. Harold jumped off and landed next to the wolf. The wolf licked Harold's ear after he stood upright.

"Hey, you gotta quit that or people are going to talk," Harold said sarcastically. Then the wolf pointed at the apocalyptic city with its nose. "You want me to go there?" The wolf nodded. "You're kidding, right? I mean, look at it. It's a freaking war zone," Harold complained, taking two steps forward. "No way—," he continued, turning around. The boat and the wolf were gone. "Of course," Harold said, clenching his teeth. "Great!"

Harold continued his profane-laced tirade as he marched towards the embattled city.

He saw a small military encampment a quarter mile away and headed in that direction. As he got closer, he saw German soldiers and vehicles everywhere. One tent in particular caught his attention. A small group of German officers and unmarked men were huddled in a highly classified briefing.

The officers wore the traditional uniforms adorned with medals and iron crosses. However the unmarked men wore non-descriptive clothing. Some had a drab poncho covering them. Most of them were unshaven and their faces were smeared with soil. Harold saw several rifles, with powerful scopes attached, hanging from their shoulders.

"Snipers," he whispered.

One man stood out from the others. His dark hair was concealed under a dark hood, but his piercing blue eyes cut through the dirt and grime covering his face.

One of the officers pointed at a map on the table. "Our planes and artillery have pounded the city night and day, but the Russians are digging in and turning it into a close-quarters battle."

"That's where you gentlemen come in," another officer said, stepping towards the table. "Our army is going street by street but is being picked off by their snipers. We need you men to take them out."

"What are your thoughts, Dietrich?" the first officer asked.

The man with the blue eyes answered, "It'll be difficult but not impossible. The Russians have some of the best marksmen in the world and they are defending their homeland."

Another officer in a black Gestapo uniform stepped up to the table. "Surely, the Russians are no match for the great Dietrich Schmidt and his Todesgeisters. Or are you becoming a communist sympathizer, Captain Schmidt?" The little man glared at Dietrich through his black-rimmed glasses.

"Before the war, I trained with the Russians and I respect them. They are good at their craft." Schmidt stared back at the Gestapo officer. "I don't have neither the time nor the patience for your politics."

"Is that so?" the Gestapo officer asked, sliding his hand towards his holster. He rested his hand on the pistol. A bead of sweat ran down the side of his face.

"Unless you want this to be your last moment on earth, I suggest you take your hand off that pistol," Schmidt said, taking a step towards the officer.

"Deeter," a unit officer warned.

"Because I will snap your neck before you unholster that weapon," Schmidt continued.

The unit commander rose from his chair. "Dietrich, stand down." At first, Schmidt didn't flinch. "That's an order, Captain!"

"Sir," Schmidt responded, stepping back and standing at attention.

"And you," the Colonel barked at the Gestapo officer. "Get out of here while you're still breathing." Visibly shaken, the little man marched out of the tent. "I should let you kill that idiot," the Colonel said to Schmidt with a smirk.

"My apologies for letting my temper get the best of me," Schmidt said.

"Nonsense, those buffoons make our jobs harder," the Colonel replied. He lit a cigarette and took in a drag. As he exhaled the smoke, he said, "Go do your jobs and take out their snipers."

"Yes sir," Schmidt answered.

"Happy hunting, gentlemen," the Colonel said. All of the men saluted as the Colonel marched out of the tent.

Schmidt waited for the other officers to leave the tent before he addressed his men. "Be careful out there. You know what to do," was all he said. Each man nodded before grabbing his rifle on the way out of the tent.

Harold and Schmidt were the last two out. Harold saw each sniper heading towards the city but on different paths. The snipers usually worked in teams consisting of two or three men. However, because of the sheer size of the city, each man was working alone on this mission.

While the battle raged on, each man easily slipped into the city unnoticed and unopposed. Hence the unit's nickname, Todesgeister or death ghost.

Dietrich was the last one to reach the ruins on the outskirts of the city. He entered an abandoned apartment building and disappeared from plain sight. He stealthily moved through the hallways like a silent wind, his rifle always at the ready. Harold was in awe of how a man his size maneuvered around like a cat, quiet and efficient.

Dietrich froze and knelt down on one knee. Harold heard the usual rumbling of battle off in the distance but other than that, it was silent. Suddenly, a squadron of German airplanes raced over the building rooftops. The empty building shook. Dietrich approached a window facing the river but stayed out of the direct line of sight. Harold was a footstep behind him.

They saw a line of Russian boats crossing the Volga river. Some of the boats were arriving with relief troops to fight, others departing the city with women and children, trying to flee the fighting. Harold cringed when he saw the German pilots open fire on the boats. Dietrich watched with no emotion.

The bodies of men, women and children were instantly torn apart, limbs and torsos flying in all directions. Some of the soldiers dove into the water in an attempt to swim away but were shot by their superiors for desertion. Women cried as they held pieces of their children in their arms.

Harold covered his mouth with his hand and watched in horror as the German planes circled back around for another pass. Some of the pilots released bombs as they showered the boats again with heavy machine gun fire. Some of the bombs missed and only exploded in the water, others found their target. Those boats disintegrated on impact. Suitcases, clothing and dismembered bodies floated on the cold river's surface.

Dietrich heard heavy troop movement on the street below. He slowly walked to the other side of the apartment and cautiously looked out the window. Harold followed and stood behind Dietrich, glancing over his shoulder. Just below them was a regiment of German soldiers creating a firing line on one side of the square. On the other side stood the Red Army.

German Panzers, large armored tanks, lined up behind the troops, aiming their guns at the Russians. The order was given and the Russians charged, running straight at the Germans. The Wehrmacht forces unleashed heavy machine gun fire upon them, cutting through the Russians. Some of the Panzers opened fire with their big shells, destroying men and buildings alike. Some of the Russian soldiers retreated only to be gunned down by their own troops.

The gunfire stopped and an eerie calm came over the square. The scent of dead bodies and gunpowder hung in the air as the smoke cleared. Some of the German soldiers raised their heads to get a better look at the outcome. A single shot rang out and a German officer's head exploded.

"Sniper!" one of the soldiers shouted below.

Dietrich dropped and belly-crawled over to a gaping hole in the wall. He positioned his rifle and peered into the scope. Russian snipers routinely shot from one location and would move to different location before taking another shot. He saw movement on the third floor of a building on the other side of the square, about three hundred yards away.

"There you are," he whispered, setting the dials on his scope.

He slowed his breathing and gently rested his finger on the trigger. Once he saw the flash of the sun's reflection off the Russian's scope, he squeezed the trigger. He absorbed the rifle's recoil with his shoulder. It reminded him he was still alive. The reflection disappeared. Dietrich patiently looked through his scope, watching the second sniper crawl away from his comrade's dead body.

For several days, Dietrich silently moved around the city, never shooting from the same location twice. Some days, he would wait patiently for hours to get the perfect shot. Other days, he moved multiple times before taking out his target. Harold followed him everywhere to watch a master at work.

After the sun went down on the fourth night out, Dietrich pulled the pancho off his head and slid backwards away from the hole in the wall. He sat up and took a quick look out the window at the area below. Once he was satisfied that everything was clear. He stood up and headed for the stairwell.

He went down the stairs and peeked out of the bombed-out door. Harold came down and stood behind Dietrich. With his rifle at the ready, Dietrich walked out and headed down the street. He and Harold stayed close and tight to the building walls as they stayed in the shadows.

A couple of blocks away, they slipped into a dark, abandoned building. Dietrich methodically climbed the stairs. At the first landing, he made a noise that sounded like a pigeon. Another pigeon sound from upstairs answered back. He relaxed, shouldered his weapon and continued walking up.

186

Harold followed him up. When they reached the second floor, Harold saw the other snipers from Dietrich's team sitting around a small fire in the far corner of the room. He noticed the windows were covered with blankets to conceal their location. Dietrich sat down in the one vacant spot of the circle around the fire.

"Gentlemen," Dietrich whispered. The men nodded back. Even though he was the ranking officer, he kept things informal. The men never addressed each other by rank, only using first names.

"Let's see what everybody has," Klaus whispered.

Each man began pulling out random items from their coats and backpacks. One man pulled out some fruit he found in a nearby shop. Another placed some candy and cigarettes on the floor in front of him. Dietrich pulled out several loaves of bread and cheese.

"Not bad," Klaus said. "Look what I found." He pulled out a tin of caviar and a bottle of vodka.

"Whoa," some of the men replied in hushed awe.

"Bon appetit," Dietrich said.

Each man shared his spoils with the others. The bottle of vodka made the rounds while the men enjoyed the bread, cheese and caviar. After the make-shift feast, some of the men enjoyed a cigarette while others had the candy for dessert.

"Klaus," Dietrich said softly. "How many?"

"Two."

Dietrich looked at the man next to Klaus. "Hans?"

"Three so far."

Each man told Dietrich how many targets they eliminated. Klaus took another swig of vodka and wiped his mouth. "How many for you, Deeter?"

Dietrich smiled. "Four."

"I win," Hans said, holding his hand out in front of Klaus.

"Damn it," Klaus whispered, slapping a pack of cigarettes onto Hans' hand. A quiet laugh broke out in the room.

"We don't want them to know we are here," Dietrich said in a serious tone. "If we're not careful, the hunters will become the prey. Stay vigilant." The men nodded in agreement. "Get some rest, I'll take first watch," he said, walking towards the stairwell. The men closed their eyes to get a few hours of much needed sleep.

Harold opened his eyes when he heard footsteps pass by his head. He sat up and rubbed the sleep from his eyes. The room was dark as the men moved around in the predawn hours. One after another, the men walked downstairs. Dietrich and Klaus watched the surrounding area from the windows. Every minute or so, another man would step out into the darkness and disappear.

Klaus stood up then paused momentarily. Once Dietrich gave him the all clear, Klaus walked downstairs and out of the building. Dietrich waited for five minutes and did the same. He and Harold walked several blocks before arriving at the destination.

Before the sun rose and lit up the dead city, the predator was already settled in his perch. Dietrich was on the floor, lying on his belly. The gaping hole in the wall gave him the perfect view of the streets below and the buildings surrounding him.

The deadly master used rubble and debris to camouflage his position. *There's no way anybody out there can see him,* Harold thought. *I'm sitting right next to him and I can barely see him.*

The sound of machine gun fire ripped through the streets as a battle erupted below. Officers shouted commands in German and Russian. Dietrich only shot when there was an explosion; it masked the sound of his rifle. He concentrated on eliminating the officers until he saw Russian tanks enter the neighborhood.

"Shit," he mumbled.

The German tanks were blocks away, in a different part of the city. The first tank fired. The round hit the street below Klaus' building. Bodies were helplessly tossed into the air like dismembered rag dolls.

Klaus placed the tank commander's head in his crosshairs. He gently squeezed the trigger. A split second later, the tank commander's head exploded. His limp body fell back inside the tank.

"Sniper!" one of the tank's crewmen shouted.

"I think it came from that building, sir," the gunner said.

"Destroy it," the tank's second-in-command ordered.

Dietrich saw the tank's gun move up. "Get out of there, Klaus," he mumbled.

Boom! The tank round hit the building's second floor, collapsing it into rubble. Dietrich swung his rifle over and stared into the scope. Klaus was pinned under a large metal beam. He was alive and reaching for his rifle, but it was out of reach.

"Charge!" a Russian officer screamed as the Germans retreated.

Dietrich shot the officer through the heart. He squeezed off two more rounds, killing two tank commanders before he jumped up and ran for the stairs. Harold ran after him. Dietrich exited the building and headed towards Klaus. He took out three more Russians as he shot on the run.

Three Russian soldiers climbed the rubble and found Klaus. "Not your lucky day. Is it, kraut?" one said, pointing his rifle at Klaus' head.

In a full sprint, Dietrich aimed and shot the Russian in the head. It was the last round in his rifle. He tossed it aside and pulled out his pistol.

Before the other two could get a shot off, Dietrich shot and killed both of them. He killed several more Russians before he ran out of ammo again. He tossed the pistol when he reached the pile of rubble.

He raced up to Klaus. "We're getting the hell out of here," he said, reaching down and placing his hands under the beam.

He grunted loudly as he lifted the heavy beam off Klaus' legs. After Klaus pulled himself out from under it, Dietrich dropped the beam.

Klaus tested his legs, trying to move them. "Fuck!" he screamed. "They're crushed, Deeter."

Dietrich picked Klaus up and threw him over his shoulder. He quickly navigated the sharp rocks and rubble down to the street. He ran several steps before he heard the gunshot.

Dietrich winced in pain when the bullet shattered his left femur. His leg gave out. He and Klaus tumbled onto the pavement. Klaus rolled over and shot the Russian with his pistol. More were coming down the street. Klaus unloaded a barrage of bullets while Dietrich tied a rag around his lame leg.

Dietrich heard Klaus moan in pain. He quickly turned around and saw a Russian soldier driving his bayonet into Klaus' chest. Dietrich pulled a knife from his belt and repeatedly stabbed the Russian in the groin. The soldier fell to his knees. Dietrich ripped the blade across the man's throat, from ear to ear.

Another Russian soldier ran over and kicked Dietrich in the face. The toe of the man's boot went directly into Dietrich's eye, causing it to rupture. Harold almost vomited when he saw the remains of Dietrich's eye hanging out of the socket.

The soldier was also shocked at the sight. Dietrich pulled out another small blade and stabbed him in the thigh. The Russian fell to one knee. Dietrich grabbed his coat and pulled him onto the ground. Like a crazed animal, Dietrich bit down hard onto the man's neck. The soldier screamed as his body convulsed. Blood squirted in all directions after Dietrich ripped the man's carotid artery out with his teeth. He spit out the chunk of tissue and collapsed on his back.

"Retreat!" a Russian commander yelled when German reinforcements arrived.

Harold was still in shock at what he had just witnessed. He regained his composure when a German walked up to Dietrich and Klaus.

"Two of our snipers, sir," a foot soldier said.

"Dear God," the German officer said, staring down at Dietrich's face.

The foot soldier placed his fingers on Klaus' neck searching for a pulse. He looked at his commander and shook his head.

"What about that one?" the officer asked, pointing at Dietrich.

The soldier place his fingers on Dietrich's neck. Dietrich grabbed his wrist and punched him in the face with other hand. The soldier fell back and grabbed his nose. "He's alive, sir."

The german officer just shook his head. "Get him some medical attention," the officer ordered.

Two other soldiers hurried a stretcher over and placed it next to Dietrich. They lifted him up carefully and placed it onto the stretcher. They waved for the medical vehicle to come forward, and as they loaded Dietrich into the back, he passed out.

Harold quickly jumped in and sat behind the medics working on Dietrich's wounds.

"We have to stop the bleeding or we'll lose the leg," one of the medics said. He glanced at Dietrich's eye. "The eye is a total loss."

"Hurry!" the other medic shouted at the driver, "Or we're going to lose him!" He applied pressure on the leg wound while the other medic applied the tourniquet.

The driver sped off and headed down the road. The medics held Dietrich's body down and braced themselves as the driver swerved back and forth dodging large holes in the streets. Harold struggled to find something to hold onto as he bounced around the back of the vehicle.

Several minutes later, they reached the field hospital on the outskirts of town. The vehicle came to an abrupt stop and the back doors flew open. Harold jumped out and moved out of the way so the medical staff could do their work. A doctor did a quick analysis of Dietrich's wounds while the Colonel watched over his shoulder.

"We can't save the leg," the doctor said to his staff. "We'll have to amputate." He did a quick assessment of Dietrich's eye. "We can't do anything for the eye, either." The medical staff took the stretcher from the medics and rushed Dietrich into the operating tent.

The Colonel grabbed the doctor's arm. "He's one of our most decorated soldiers, doctor. Do what you can to save him, Der Fuhrer is monitoring his status closely."

"Yes sir," the doctor replied. "We'll stabilize him for the airlift to Berlin."

"Good," the Colonel responded.

The doctor ran inside to start the operation. Harold stayed outside of the medical tent.

"Holy shit, Hitler's keeping tabs on him," he mumbled, scratching his head in confusion. "How come I've never heard or read about this guy before?"

Chapter 16

Harold opened his eyes when he heard movement in the room. A nurse was switching out IV bottles next to Dietrich's bed. She placed the empty bottle on a cart and walked over to the foot of the bed. She pulled the clipboard from the hook and began jotting notes.

The door opened and two doctors entered the room.

"Doctors," the young nurse said, handing the clipboard to one of the doctors.

"How's our patient today?" one doctor asked, rhetorically.

The nurse took a step back when the doctors stepped to the side of the bed. One of the doctors placed his fingers on Dietrich's neck.

Harold chuckled. "I wouldn't do that if I were you," he mumbled.

Suddenly, Dietrich opened his one good eye and grabbed the doctor by the throat. The doctor tried to pull away, but he couldn't escape Dietrich's iron grip. The other doctor grabbed Dietrich's arm with both hands and pulled with all his might, but no luck. The captive doctor's eyes rolled back into his head and he passed out. Dietrich released his grip and the doctor fell limp onto the floor.

"Captain Schmidt, please calm down," the nurse pleaded.

Dietrich had bloodlust in his eyes, as if he was going to kill anything near him. The other doctor ran out of the room while the nurse kept her distance. Before Dietrich ripped out his IV's and tried to get out of bed, a soldier ran into the room and pushed him back.

"Deeter, it's me, Hans!" the soldier shouted. "You're safe. You're in a hospital in Berlin."

Dietrich stared at Hans for a few seconds. "Hans?"

"Yes sir, you're okay," Hans reassured him. Two soldiers with guns drawn came into the room. Hans turned and waved them off.

"It's okay, gentlemen. He calmed down," the nurse said. "Please help with the doctor."

The two soldiers holstered their pistols and helped the nurse pick the doctor up from the floor.

"What happened?" another doctor asked the nurse as they walked out of the room.

After the door closed behind them, Hans looked back at Dietrich.

Dietrich slowed his breathing and relaxed. "What happened, Hans? Where's Klaus?"

"Klaus is gone, Deeter."

Dietrich closed his eye. "I failed him."

"You did what you could. Instead of being taken prisoner and tortured, he died fighting. It was an honorable death," Hans said.

"I should be dead, not him," Dietrich answered with a sense of guilt. He reached over and touched the bandage covering his other eye. "My eye?"

"It's gone, my friend," Hans replied. Dietrich sat up and looked at his legs. He only saw the impression of one leg under the sheets. "Unfortunately, they couldn't save the leg either. You lost too much blood and they had to apply a tourniquet."

"What good is a soldier with only one eye and one leg?" Dietrich asked.

"Hey," Hans said, placing his hand on Dietrich's shoulder. "At least you're alive, Deeter."

Dietrich lied back in his bed and said nothing. A minute later, he turned towards Hans. "Why are you here, Hans?"

Hans chuckled. "They thought a familiar face would help you transition to your new assignment. And, I'm supposed to keep you from killing the staff."

Harold laughed and Dietrich actually cracked a smile.

"New assignment?" Dietrich asked.

"Headquarters is sending a Gestapo officer over to brief you on it," Hans said.

"Gestapo?"

"Yep."

"Assholes," Dietrich growled.

"Yep," Hans agreed. The door to the room opened. Hans watched the Gestapo officer walking in. "Ah, speak of the devil." He looked back at Dietrich. "I'll be right outside. Don't kill this one," he whispered to Dietrich.

"No promises," Dietrich whispered back.

Hans smiled and walked past the officer. "He's all yours."

The officer goose-stepped over to Dietrich's bed. His riding boots left scuff marks on the white floor. "It's an honor to meet you, Major Schmidt," the officer said, taking his hat off. Not a follicle of his blond hair moved.

"It's Captain," Dietrich responded.

"Not anymore, sir. You've been promoted for your heroics on the battlefield in Stalingrad," the officer said, sitting down on the chair next to Dietrich's bed.

"But I heard we lost the city to the Russians."

"We did," the officer agreed. "But your bravery is a rallying cry for our men on the eastern front to keep up the good fight."

Propaganda speak, Dietrich thought while he listened to the Gestapo officer's replies. "Well, I'm no use to you now," Dietrich said, pointing to his eye and then his leg.

"Perhaps not against the Russians or the Americans, but the motherland has other enemies." The officer pulled an envelope from his coat pocket. He handed it to Dietrich and stood up. "Der Fuhrer still sees you as a valuable asset, Major."

Dietrich took the letter and glared at the officer. The officer goose-stepped out of the room.

Harold jumped out of his chair when he saw the pale-white girl with blood-red eyes standing where the Gestapo officer had just been a few seconds before.

"Oh shit," he cried out.

Dietrich didn't flinch when he saw the little girl's evil smile. He calmly held out his hand and waited. The little girl extended her arm and placed two rings in his palm. He sat up and stared at them as she floated out of the room.

Dietrich closed his fist and wiped a tear from his eye. He placed the rings on the table next to the bed before opening the envelope. He carefully read his new orders and promotion documents.

"Auschwitz?"

Chapter 17

After months of healing and getting used to his prosthetic leg, it was time for Dietrich to report to his new assignment. He, along with Harold and Hans, stood by the tracks of the central station waiting for the train. The two snipers wore the dark gray uniform of the Wehrmacht officers, but the number of combat medals on their uniforms made them stand out on the crowded platform.

Many of the young soldiers stared in awe at the two war horses. "Todesgeist," one young soldier whispered to his comrade. They both gazed at the insignia on the snipers' lapel.

"They think you look like a pirate from an Errol Flynn movie, Deeter," Hans said, referring to Dietrich's black eye patch.

"Fuck you," Dietrich replied with a smile. Hans and Harold laughed. The Gestapo officer marched towards them. "You've got to be kidding me. This asshole?"

"Looks like your babysitter has arrived," Hans added.

"Good morning, Major Schmidt. I'll be accompanying you to your next assignment."

Hans looked up when he heard the boarding call for his train. "That's my train," he said, extending his hand out. "Farewell for now, Deeter."

Dietrich shook his hand and then hugged Hans. "Thank you for everything, my friend," he said.

Each man took a step back. "Don't kill anybody before you get there," Hans said, picking his bag up from the ground. Dietrich just nodded.

Hans turned and disappeared into the crowd.

"After you, Major," the Gestapo officer said, waiting at the train door.

Dietrich gathered himself and used his cane to walk to the train. Even with a very noticeable limp, his presence alone commanded respect. It took a minute for him to get up the steps and walk into the car. As he walked down the aisle to his cabin, each soldier stood at attention and saluted the war hero.

"You see, Major?" the officer said, walking in after Dietrich and sitting across from him. "The men respect you. You are a folk hero to them."

"I am no hero," Dietrich disagreed.

"What you did in Stalingrad is the stuff of legends, Major. It was extraordinary, super human," the officer expounded with pride.

Harold walked in and sat down next to Dietrich. He could tell that Dietrich didn't like all of this attention by the way he ground his jaw.

"Please," Dietrich said, struggling to keep his temper. "Let's just be quiet for the trip."

"As you wish, sir," the officer replied. He pulled a book out of his bag and began reading.

Dietrich leaned his head back and closed his eyes as the train jolted forward. Harold stared out the window as the train picked up speed. Soon, they were outside of Berlin, heading east. Harold sat back and watched the countryside fly by outside.

Several hours later, Dietrich began mumbling in his sleep. Then he started violently whipping his head back and forth, left to right. He was breathing heavily and his mumbling grew louder. The Gestapo officer looked up from his book and calmly rested his hand on his pistol.

Suddenly, Dietrich's eye opened wide and he shouted, "No!" He stood up and looked around the cabin in confusion. He glared at the officer. "What's going on?"

"You had a bad dream, Major," the officer responded, sliding his hand away from the pistol. "It happens to many men who have seen a lot of combat."

"My apologies," Dietrich said, gathering himself and sitting back down.

"No offense taken, sir," the officer replied. He checked his watch and looked out the window. "We'll arrive in Auschwitz in a few hours. Would you like to join me for lunch?"

"Thank you, but I think I'll stay here and rest," Dietrich said.

The officer nodded and clicked his heels before exiting the cabin.

Harold woke up when the train came to an abrupt stop. He rubbed his eyes and looked around the cabin. Dietrich and the officer were standing and adjusting their uniforms.

"Ready, Major?" the officer asked.

"Yes," Dietrich answered reluctantly.

They both put their hats on and stepped out into the crowded aisle. "Make way, officers on deck!" one of the soldiers shouted. The men either pressed themselves against the wall or hurried to get out of the way.

"Thank you," Dietrich said, walking down the aisle with his cane. As he went by, each soldier stood at attention and saluted him.

Harold followed the two officers to the car door and stepped out onto the ramp. An SS officer approached them as soon as they disembarked from the train.

"Major Schmidt, let me introduce you to the camp Commandant, Colonel Schafer."

"Pleasure to meet you, sir," Dietrich said, saluting the colonel.

"The pleasure is mine, Major Schmidt. Your reputation of hero precedes you."

"Just doing my job, sir."

"If only I had twenty more of you, the camp would run like a well-oiled machine," the colonel said with a hearty laugh.

Seriously, why haven't I ever heard of this guy? Harold thought.

The Gestapo officer handed the colonel a manilla envelope full of documents. "Thank you. Here are the camp reports for Der Fuhrer," the colonel said, handing the officer a briefcase.

"Thank you, sir," the officer said, saluting the colonel. He turned and faced Dietrich. "Good luck, Major Schmidt, our journey ends here." He shook Dietrich's hand.

"Oh," Dietrich responded surprised. "Where are you going?"

"I'm going back to Berlin," the officer said, marching back up the steps and into the car.

Dietrich bent over to pick his bags up. "My driver will get those for you, Major. Please leave them," the colonel said.

The colonel's driver ran over and fetched Dietrich's luggage and promptly placed it in the trunk of the car. He ran over and opened the back door for the colonel. The colonel climbed in and claimed his seat on the far side of the vehicle.

"Major," the driver said, pointing at the seat next to the colonel. Dietrich nodded and carefully climbed in. The driver closed the door behind Dietrich and ran to the other side of the car, jumping into the driver's seat. Harold quickly opened the door and leapt in before the driver sped off.

On the way, Colonel Schafer went over the camp's procedures and specifications.

"If I may ask, sir, what kind of camp is this?" Dietrich innocently asked.

"A prison camp."

A pungent scent hung in the air as they arrived. "What is that?" Dietrich asked, covering his nose with his hand.

"You'll get used to it, Major," the Colonel answered, sporting a sinister grin. The SS guards saluted when the car drove through the iron gate of the camp entrance. "Welcome to Auschwitz," the colonel hissed with pleasure.

Dietrich read the words on the gate above them. *Arbeit Macht Frei.* "Work sets you free," he mumbled.

As they drove past the barracks, the colonel looked at Dietrich. "This is Auschwitz One," the colonel said, pointing at the rows of brick buildings. "We keep our Polish prisoners here." He tapped the driver on the shoulder. "Take us to Birkenau. A fresh batch of prisoners just arrived."

"Yes sir," the soldier answered, continuing down the muddy road.

"Birkenau is phase two," the colonel said to Dietrich. "That's where the magic happens." He gave a sadistic chuckle. The car pulled up next to the rail ramp. Steam bellowed from the locomotive's underbelly.

Boxcars? Dietrich thought, gazing at the long line down the track.

"Come on, Major," the colonel said, getting out of the car. "You'll get a first-hand look at our operations."

The SS soldiers saluted them as Dietrich and the colonel took their place next to the first car. Three to four SS officers stood by the door of each boxcar. They tapped their riding crops against their legs, waiting in anticipation.

Dietrich counted ten to fifteen pairs of K-9 soldiers. The German Shepherds were already barking and foaming at the mouth. He noticed the guard towers alongside the tracks with more soldiers pointing machine guns at the rail cars.

Holy shit, what's in those cars? Dietrich wondered, taking it all in.

The colonel raised his hand and gave the signal. An officer at each car unlocked the door handle and pulled the doors open. The officers yelled and berated the people walking out on the ramp. The K-9 soldiers came closer, terrorizing the poor people huddled together in panic.

The pit of Dietrich's stomach ached when he saw women and children exiting the rail cars. "Sir, I don't understand," he said. "These are non-combatants. They're innocents."

The colonel was delighted with all of the chaos surrounding them. "Don't be fooled, Major. They are the enemy of the Third Reich."

A man fell on the ground. One of the K-9 soldiers released his dog. The man pleaded in pain as the dog ripped his leg apart. The German soldier casually walked over and shot the man in the head before he retrieved his dog.

"Who are they?" Dietrich asked, trying to make sense of everything.

"Jews," the colonel growled with hatred.

A woman stumbled near the colonel. He marched over and forcefully kicked her in the stomach. She groaned as she held her stomach and fell to the ground. He motioned for one of the soldiers to come and drag her away. She screamed in fear as the soldier pulled her away by her hair.

The colonel looked back at Dietrich. "These vermin are a plague. They need to be wiped off the face of the earth."

"This isn't right," Dietrich mumbled. "There is no honor in this."

Harold just watched in horror. He had read about the holocaust, but it was totally different seeing it firsthand.

The colonel pulled out a handkerchief and wiped his boot off. After he was satisfied that the smudge was gone, he walked back over to Dietrich.

"Let me show you the prisoner barracks. Follow me," he said, walking away from the rail platform. They approached a set of buildings. "The men are housed here," he added, pointing as they walked by. "The women and children are in these buildings."

With each step, rage and despair grew inside Dietrich. Harold noticed movement out of the corner of his eye. He gasped when he saw the pale-white girl with blood-red eyes walking beside them. She stared at Harold and smiled, exposing her razor-sharp fangs. Harold blinked and she disappeared.

"Where did she go?" he wondered, frantically looking around for her.

"Come," the colonel said, gesturing at the dark building ahead. "This is the pinnacle of efficiency."

Dietrich flinched when he felt a burning sensation in his coat pocket. He stopped, reached into his pocket and pulled out the two rings. "No, please no. Not here," he whispered, staring at the glowing rings.

"Oh my god," Harold said, stopping in his tracks.

Dietrich saw people lined up alongside the dark building. They looked more like zombies than human beings. Only a very thin layer of skin covered their skeletal frames. Some were infested with lice and other parasites. Others were severely beaten and their heads were shaved.

"Come, Major," the colonel said, looking back at Dietrich.

The rings began to pulsate as men got closer. The soldier gave the signal for the people to disrobe. Slowly, they obeyed and began shedding their clothing. Harold wept as he witnessed one of humanity's darkest hours.

A young bald woman was too weak to move and fell to the ground. After months of repeatedly being raped and beaten by the SS guards, her frail body had given up. The German soldier shouted at her and nudged her with his boot, but she couldn't move. She only had enough energy to lift her head from the mud and glance at Dietrich.

"My love," he whispered when he saw her hazel eyes. The gray skies turned red when he unleashed his rampage. Dietrich marched over and pulled the colonel's pistol out of his holster.

"What the hell do you think you're doing!" the colonel shouted.

Dietrich pistol-whipped him across the face. The colonel fell to the ground like a lump of bricks and laid there, stunned. Before the soldier could react, Dietrich put two rounds into his forehead. Harold heard the alarm go off and soldiers running towards them.

Dietrich sat on the ground next to the young lady. He carefully wrapped his arms around her and held her close to him. "I'm so sorry," he whispered to her.

With her last ounce of life, she looked up at him and smiled. "I love you," was the last thing she said before she died in his arms.

Dietrich sobbed as he held her tightly.

Harold jumped when he heard the gunshot. The bullet entered Dietrich's back and exploded out of his chest. He continued holding the girl close to him. Another shot, the bullet severed his spine and he lost the use of his limbs from the neck down.

The colonel walked over and stared down at Dietrich. He rubbed his bloody cheek as he glared at the traitor. He picked his pistol up off the ground and pointed it at Dietrich's head as Dietrich took his last breath.

"Jew lover," the colonel mumbled as he squeezed the trigger.

"No!" Harold yelled when the round went into Dietrich's head. He fell to his knees.

"Throw them in the oven," the colonel said. He turned towards the camp's political officer. "This man never existed."

"Sir?" the political officer asked.

"Burn his body, destroy all of his records. I want no memory of him, no mention of him in history books. Got it?" the colonel added.

"Yes sir," the political officer answered. He marched off to make phone calls to Berlin.

The soldiers began taking Dietrich's uniform off. "Leave it on," the colonel ordered. "No evidence."

"Yes sir," they replied.

Two soldiers picked the young lady up and carried her to the crematorium. Two more soldiers grabbed Dietrich's arms and dragged his body through the mud. Once inside, they crammed the two bodies into the oven and started the fire. They walked back out and continued shouting at the poor souls lined up outside the other building.

Harold quietly sat in the mud for hours. He was numb from everything he witnessed. He raised his head when he saw a tiny silhouette floating towards the crematorium. He stood up and followed it in. When he entered, he saw the pale-white girl, sifting through Dietrich's and the young lady's ashes.

What the hell is she doing? he wondered.

She dug her talons into the ash for a few seconds before she found her prize. She pulled an object out and blew on it. It was one of the rings. She reached in again and found the other. She placed them in her pocket and looked at Harold.

He shielded his eyes and took a step back when the bright light engulfed the room.

Chapter 18

Before Harold opened his eyes, he noticed that the smell of death was gone. He inhaled fresh mountain air and opened his eyes. The large wolf was keeping a watchful eye on the waters ahead from the boat's bow. Harold quietly sat on the deck.

The wolf looked back at him. Harold continued staring at the deck of the boat beneath him. The amount of death he saw on the journey weighed heavily on him. The wolf walked back and sat in front of Harold. Harold looked up with a blank stare. "No more, please. I can't do this anymore." The wolf nodded and returned to his perch on the bow.

The waters were calm. The sky was dark and gray. No clouds, no birds, just sorrow. It was eerily quiet except for an unusual hum that grew louder as they went along.

"What the hell is that noise?" Harold wondered, standing up for a better look.

The scenery around him was dark, forbidding yet surprisingly beautiful. They were crossing a lake nestled between two great mountains. The trees on both mountains were full of leaves which weren't the usual green color, but more of a lighter shade of gray, dull but uniquely amazing in their own way.

There was no sun in the sky but everything was clear and vivid. Harold saw a cabin on the shore. He noticed the trees around the small dwelling, long, lifeless branches that disappeared into the melancholy sky and stretched for miles on both sides. He squinted to get a better look at the objects sitting on the branches.

What kind of birds are those?

The humming continued to grow louder the closer they got to the cabin. It was now affecting Harold physically and he felt nauseous. The wolf howled loudly one time. Everything shook as the howl echoed across the landscape, ripples shooting out across the water. Harold almost lost his balance and grabbed the side of the boat.

The humming suddenly stopped; silence swept over the land. The large objects on the branches began to slightly sway back and forth, staring at the approaching boat.

As they came closer to shore, Harold could see that the objects on the branches weren't birds, they were human-like. Their bodies were large and black, almost devoid of shape. However, their faces were pale and contorted as if they were gripped with pain. Their eyes were cold and black.

The boat beached and came to a complete stop on the dark sand. The wolf jumped off and waited for Harold to join it. Harold looked at the beings in the trees and then back at the wolf. The wolf motioned for him to follow it. Reluctantly, Harold came ashore and followed the wolf towards the cabin.

The tree beings glared at Harold and groaned as he walked by them. Some whispered as they seemingly stared through his soul. The wolf growled, silencing the whispers. Harold quickened his pace to stay close to the wolf.

The wolf climbed the wooden steps leading up to the porch. Harold paused and waited at the base of the stairs as the wolf walked towards the closed door. He was startled when the wolf stepped into the closed door and vanished. Before he could mutter a word, the door slowly opened. A large black man with piercing blue eyes stepped out on the porch.

"Uncle Alex?" Harold asked in disbelief.

"Hey, Harry. The beard looks good on you." Harold was at a loss for words. "You're just in time for dinner. Come in, come in," Alex stepped back into the cabin. Harold was a little apprehensive at first, but entered the cabin. "Cop a squat," Alex said, pointing at a small wooden table next to the kitchen. He saw the look of confusion in Harold's eyes. "You have questions."

"That's an understatement," Harold responded.

Alex smiled. "I'll tell you everything over dinner. You have my word."

"Okay," Harold agreed, walking over and sitting at the table.

Alex pulled two bowls out from the cupboard and filled them with beef stew. He walked over to the table and set one of the bowls in front of Harold. Alex tried handing a spoon to Harold, but he was staring out the window at the creatures in the trees.

"Here," Alex said, tapping Harold on the shoulder with the spoon.

"Thanks," Harold said.

Alex sat down. He brought a spoonful of hot stew up to his mouth and blew on it. "Fire away, Harry. I'll answer your questions."

"Where the hell are we?"

"Some call it Purgatory, others call it Limbo. I call it my hunting cabin in Norway from when I was a boy." Alex consumed a mouthful of stew.

"Why here?"

Alex wiped his mouth. "That, I don't know. I woke up here right after I fell into the coma. But don't worry," Alex added, knocking on the table, "she can't rack us down here."

"Who's she?" Harold asked.

"The Mesopotamians called her Nergal. My people called her Hel. You know her as Death."

"Wait, what?" Harold was in disbelief.

"The pale-white girl with blood-red eyes," Alex added, taking in another mouthful of stew.

"Oh shit," Harold mumbled, trying to wrap his mind around it. He quickly looked out the window when the tree creatures began to moan loudly again.

"Don't worry about them either, they can't hurt you," Alex said reassuringly.

"Who are they?"

"Those are all of the souls I've replaced over the centuries," Alex responded with a sense of guilt.

"I don't understand," Harold said.

"I'll start from the beginning," Alex said, putting his spoon on the table. "My original name is Ulfr, son of Gustav."

"The viking I saw die?" Harold frantically asked.

"Yes," Alex replied. "That was my first life. I was also Lambert, Dietrich and many others."

"Are you kidding me?" Harold shouted, jumping up from his chair. "Don't mess with me!"

"It's the truth, Harry," Alex said in a calming tone. "I've never lied to you before, right?"

He's right, Harold thought. *He always tells me the truth, no matter how bad it is.* "Right," Harold said, taking a deep breath and sitting back down.

Alex's eyes began to tear up. "When I lost Frida in England, Hel found a way to entice me to do her bidding. She promised I would see Frida again if I agreed to kill for her. One of the few things I'm really good at," Alex said, wiping his eyes. "I did it all for love, Harry.

"Oh my god," Harold gasped. "The Muslim woman Lambert tried to save, and the Jewish girl Dietrich died for were—"

"Yes, it was Frida each time," Alex sadly replied. Harold's eyes filled with tears. "I do get to see Frida in every life, but Hel left out the part where I can never save her in time and I am forced to watch her die, every time."

"That's horrible," Harold said with tears running down his cheeks. "Is that what happened with Mrs. Jaworski from the flower shop? She was Frida?"

"Yes," Alex responded. "I thought we got one over on Hel because we found each other and didn't watch each other die. Or so I thought," Alex said, looking down at the stew. "Those inbred bastards saw us together one night and decided to hang her from a tree the next day. They wrote 'nigger lover' on her body and beat her before they killed her."

Harold felt the rage in Alex's voice and watched it play across his face. "They laughed when I found them in the woods. Well, you saw what happened," Alex said, referring to the crime scene photos.

"Yeah, but I understand why you did it, Uncle Alex," Harold said. "I would've done the same thing. Any man would."

"I wanted to tell somebody my story before I leave this life," Alex said. "What's weird is that Hel doesn't know I'm here."

"Really?" Harold asked.

"Yeah," Alex replied. "Since I'm in a coma, I'm neither alive nor dead, I'm something in between. I guess she can't see me in that realm."

"Oh wow," Harold said looking at Alex's eyes.

"What?" Alex asked.

"I've been so self-absorbed over the past several years, I never noticed that we have the same colored eyes until now."

"It runs in our family," Alex told him.

"But we're not related."

"Oh, we are," Alex answered. Harold was perplexed. "You are a direct descendant of my brother Henrik."

"That's impossible," Harold countered.

"Look at your last name, Harry, *Gustafson*. The spelling changed a bit over the centuries but it means son of Gustaf or Gustav, our father."

"No way," Harold denied.

"I wasn't able to bear children, but my brother Henrik had many children and they had children, and so on. Why do you think I was such a close friend of your dad's?"

"So in a weird, convoluted way, you're my great, great, however many, uncle?"

"Yes."

"Wow," Harold said, letting it soak in. "That's mind-blowing."

"You're the closest thing I've ever had to a son. I wanted you to know my story," Alex said.

"I don't know what to say, I'm honored," Harold said. "What do I call you? Ulfr? Lambert?"

"Uncle Alex is good," Alex answered with a smile.

Suddenly, the souls in the trees began to moan and wail loudly. They violently thrashed around, causing the branches to sway back and forth.

"What's going on?" Harold asked.

"I don't know," Alex said.

They looked out the window and saw dark clouds rolling across the lake, coming towards them. Bolts of lightning shot out across the sky, striking the lake and the surrounding trees. The souls went into a frenzy when some of the bolts struck one of the trees of souls. Branches fell and the souls tumbled to the ground below.

The earth and sky shook as the clouds came closer. The wind whipped through the cabin. The whistling sound was deafening.

"Stay here," Alex said, grabbing an ax by the door and stepping outside.

Harold heard the sound of hooves getting louder and louder. It sounded like a large cavalry was attacking. Then, all at once, it stopped. Harold could hear his own heartbeat through the silence.

Harold held his breath when he heard a woman's voice. "At last, I found you."

Harold ran to the door and pulled it open. He shielded his eyes from a blinding light and was thrown back into the cabin. "Uncle Alex!" he shouted as he hit the floor.

Chapter 19

Harold leapt up from his chair and stumbled backwards until he fell on the floor.

"Whoa, whoa, whoa, Harry," Wendy said, trying to calm him down.

Harold stood back up and glared at Wendy like a wounded animal backed into a corner. "Where am I?" he demanded.

"The hospital?" Wendy replied with some confusion. "Have you been drinking?"

"What year is this?" Harold continued.

"What?"

Harold's vision was clear now. He quickly looked around the room and saw Alex lying on the hospital bed. *I don't understand,* he thought when he saw Alex hooked up to the respirator, heart monitor and various other machines.

"Harold, it's me, Wendy," she said. "What happened?"

Harold looked down at his clothes. *They're clean,* he thought. He reached up and touched his face. "Where's my beard?" he asked, running to the bathroom mirror.

Wendy saw the haunted look in his eyes when he stared at his reflection. He was looking for a rational explanation, but couldn't come up with one.

Harold stepped out of the bathroom. "My beard's gone. My clothes are clean and I don't smell like a dead animal," Harold said, sitting back down into the chair. He looked up at Wendy. "How long was I out?"

Wendy knelt down next to him. "Only a few minutes." Harold had a bewildered expression on his face. "The guys outside said you walked in a few minutes before I did, Harry."

"But I was gone for years, decades," Harold replied, covering his face with his hands.

"You're not making any sense," Wendy said, rubbing Harold's hand.

The room door opened and the on-duty nurse came in. She saw Harold's body sunk in the chair. "You need to eat, Harry. Why don't you two go get a bite to eat and some coffee. I'll stay and keep an eye on your uncle."

"Okay," Harold said reluctantly, trying to get his wits about him.

"Thank you," Wendy whispered to the nurse as they walked out.

They walked out of the ICU ward and down to the cafeteria. At first, Harold shunned off any food offered to him by the cooking staff.

"You need to eat and keep your strength up," Wendy said with a maternal tone. Harold gave in and grabbed a turkey sandwich and some fruit.

After paying the cashier for the food, they sat down at a table in the corner of the dining hall.

"What's going on, Harry? You okay?"

"I guess it really was a dream," Harold said.

"Tell me about it," Wendy prompted, curiously.

"At the beginning, I was in a Viking village where I met Ulfr and Henrik," Harold started but was quickly interrupted by Wendy.

"Wait. The sons of Gustav, Ulfr the Destroyer and Henrik the Red?"

"Yeah," Harold responded. "I was with them in Norway and then when they went to England."

"Why on earth would you dream about something like that?" Wendy inquired. "Did you read about them or something?"

"No, I've never heard of their names before," Harold replied.

"They were two of the most vicious and well-respected Vikings in history," Wendy said, admiring the brothers. "Even the berserkers were afraid of them. Their accomplishments on the battlefield were legendary." Wendy had a puzzled look on her face. "I never found out why they called Henrik 'The Red' when he had dark black hair."

"Because he was always covered in blood during the battle," Harold answered nonchalantly, taking a bite from his sandwich.

Wendy reached into her purse and pulled out a pen and a small spiral notebook. She hurriedly wrote some notes on a blank page. "I never thought of that," she said, scribbling away.

Harold proceeded to tell her about his time with the Norsemen. She hung onto his every word. She was learning things that weren't printed in any books. He finished the story with Ulfr's fall in battle and Hel enticing him to kill for her.

"Wait," Wendy said, trying to catch up with her notes. "Hel? The goddess of death?"

"Yes," Harry answered.

"How did you know it was her?"

"Uncle Alex told me."

Wendy stopped writing and looked at Harold. "Okay, now I'm totally confused."

"I'll get to that part later," Harold said. He then told her about the two rings and what Alex told him about the eternal curse. He continued. "Then, I traveled to Jerusalem with Godfrey, Lambert and the other crusaders."

"Godfrey, the Frankish prince?" Wendy asked.

"Yes."

"Lambert? There isn't a lot of information about him," Wendy said.

"He was Godfrey's best and most noble knight," Harold said with pride. He continued telling Wendy all of the minute details of the siege of Jerusalem, Godfrey's ceremony, Lambert riding to the frail Muslim woman and Lambert's death. "My heart sank when he couldn't save her."

Tears welled up in Wendy's eyes. Not only was it a sad story, but she also felt Harold's sorrow. His sadness slightly turned into anger when he told her about the Englishman killing Lambert. Then, to fear when Hel came to claim the rings. Wendy rode the roller coaster of emotions with him.

Wendy smiled at an elderly couple sitting down at the table several feet away from them. "They're so sweet," she said, admiring the old lovebirds. She looked back at Harold. "Then what?"

"Then, I was in Stalingrad with a German sniper, Dietrich Schmidt," Harold said before taking another bite of his sandwich.

"The Todesgeister," Wendy said with smile. "Those guys were bad asses, but I've never heard of a Dietrich Schmidt."

Harold chuckled. "Yeah, they were." He continued telling her about Dietrich being severely wounded and being transferred to Auschwitz, finding the barely alive Jewish girl, and dying trying to protect her from the SS.

Wendy wiped another tear from her eye. "That's horrible and beautiful at the same time," she said.

"After that, I talked with Uncle Alex in his hunting cabin," Harold said.

"Oh, did you go there as a kid?"

"No, I didn't know he had one," Harold answered. "He told me about Hel's curse and about his soulmate, Frida."

"Wow, that dream is all over the place," Wendy said. "I'm still trying to figure out why you dreamt about so many different times, places and people."

"Alex told me that those were just three of his past lives," Harold said. "He had lived for centuries, going from one body to another."

Wendy's eyes were wide open. "That's mind-blowing, Harry. That's one helluva good story. I am impressed."

"Oh, I didn't make it up."

"Then how do you explain the dream?" Wendy asked.

"I don't know," Harold responded with some frustration.

The old couple next to them spoke to each other in German. The old man was trying to look something up on his smartphone and his wife was telling him that he didn't know what he was doing.

Harold looked over and asked in German, "Need some help?"

"Yes, thank you," the old man replied. "What part of Germany are you from?"

"I've never been," Harold answered.

"Where did you learn how to speak German so well?" the old woman asked.

Harold grinned. "An old friend taught me." He looked at Wendy with a surprised expression. "Holy shit, I can speak German."

"Okay?" Wendy responded in a perplexed tone.

"You don't understand, I didn't speak a word before I had the dream," Harold added. Wendy was speechless. Harold chuckled. "I can also speak Old Norse and Frankish." He laughed as the words raced through his mind.

"Here you go," the old man said, handing the phone over to Harold.

Harold looked it over and then showed the old couple the screen. "If you type in the address on this line and push go, it'll show the best way to get there. Do you have the address?"

The old man nodded and pulled a small slip of paper from his pocket. He read the address to Harold and he typed it in. He showed the couple again and warned them about the road construction on that side of town.

"Thank you so much, young man. If you and your wife come to Heidelberg, you are more than welcome to stay at our house," the old woman said.

"Oh, she's not my wife," Harold said, blushing a little.

"Well, not yet," the old man said with a wink.

"Don't let her get away, she's beautiful with a kind soul," the old woman added.

"I won't, promise," Harold whispered. The old couple stood up and hugged Harold and Wendy. "Take care," Harold said as they walked away.

"How is that possible?" Wendy asked, trying to rationally explain Harold's newfound knowledge of languages.

"I guess I picked it up in my time there." Harold paused and he widened his eyes. "Wait a minute. Ulfr, that's Old Norse for wolf!"

"Yeah. So?" Wendy asked.

Harold couldn't contain his excitement. He laughed out loud. "Ulfr," he said, looking at Wendy.

"Yeah?"

"Why didn't I see it before?" Harold asked. "He's the wolf, the wolf is him!" Wendy was still confused. "Don't you see? He was guiding me through the underworld!" He jumped from his chair. He stopped and looked at Wendy. "You believe me, right?"

"It's a fantastic dream, it really is, Harry. I just have a hard time believing that any of it was real," Wendy said.

"Okay, then how do you explain me speaking several languages now?"

"I don't have a good answer for that yet," Wendy replied.

"Ha," Harold said, pointing at her.

"Okay, you got me there," Wendy surrendered.

"I want to say bye to Alex on our way out," Harold said.

"Okay," Wendy said, standing up from her chair.

The two of them walked back down the hall towards Alex's hospital room.

"How's it going, guys?" Harold asked the guards as they walked up to the door.

"Pretty good, Harry. How you doing?" one of the guards opened the door for Harold and Wendy.

Wendy jumped when they heard loud squawks coming from Alex's bed. *Those sound familiar,* Harold thought, pulling the curtain aside.

"Oh!" Wendy gasped when she saw two large ravens perched on the headboard above Alex's head.

"It's you two," Harold said, recognizing the birds from his dream. He turned towards Wendy. "Those are the two ravens from my dream."

"Their names are Hugin and Munin. They are my messengers," a deep, loud voice boomed from behind them.

Harold and Wendy quickly turned around to face an extremely large Viking standing in the room with them.

He was easily seven feet tall and built like a mountain. His trousers were stretched tight across his tree-trunk-like legs. Several large hammers and knives were harnessed to his belt around his waist. The chain mail under his furs expanded and contracted with each breath, barely containing his massive torso. His arms were like pillars of ancient stone that could tear apart mortal men. His long white beard and hair flowed and intertwined with the fur on his shoulders.

Harold took in a deep breath when he looked into the giant's right eye. He could see the other side of the universe in it.

"The AllFather," Wendy whispered in awe.

"Odin?" Harold mumbled.

"They told me a lot about you, Harold," Odin said. His voice shook the building with every word. Harold was at a loss for words. He thought his heart was going to beat out of his chest. "I wanted to come and thank you personally."

"For what?" Harold asked, struggling with his words.

"After he was taken by Hel, Hildr searched heaven and earth for him." The Norse god continued. "He reached out to you and we were able to find him through you." Odin rubbed his beard. "What Hel did was unforgivable and she paid dearly for it," he said, tapping his finger on one of the large hammers.

"Is he finally going to Valhalla?" Harold asked.

Odin smiled. "He'll be eating at my table tonight."

Harold felt a sense of peace like he had never experienced before. His mind and heart calmed and he felt euphoric for his uncle Alex. "Thank you," he said to the Norse god.

Odin reached into his pocket and pulled something out. "He wanted you to have these," he said, placing the two rings in Harold's hand. Harold and Wendy stared at the glowing iron rings. "That was Hel's downfall," Odin said.

Harold looked up at him. "The rings?"

"No, Harold. Love," Odin said.

"I don't understand," Harold mumbled.

"Love without measure is the most powerful thing in the universe," Odin said. "No rules, laws or gods can match its power. It inspires men to reach beyond their potential and do magnificent things. Ulfr's love for Frida helped him deal with unspeakable horrors and he never gave up, he kept fighting. It's the same love that flows through you two."

"Thank you," Wendy said, smiling at Odin.

"I don't know what to say." Harold said.

"Honor Ulfr's memory and go do great things together," Odin said to the couple.

"We will," Harold replied.

Odin nodded his mighty head in approval. He looked over at the two ravens. "Come on, boys." The birds flew over and perched on Odin's massive shoulders. "Food and drink awaits."

Harold and Wendy blinked and the mighty god was gone. Wendy looked at Harold. "Holy shit, you were telling the truth."

Harold smiled. "Told ya."

Suddenly, Alex's heart monitor showed a flatline. The ICU staff rushed in to tend to him. "Please wait outside," one of the nurses said, ushering the couple out.

Chapter 20

A flight attendant tapped Harold on the shoulder. He glanced up from his laptop and pulled the earbud from his ear. "Please store your laptop and put your tray up, sir. We're starting our descent into Oslo."

"Sure, no problem," Harold replied. He closed up his computer and placed the earbuds in the side pocket of his bag. He glanced over and saw Wendy looking at him with an analytical expression. "What?" he asked, touching his forehead. "Do I have something on my face?"

"Nope," Wendy said, continuing to stare at him. She came to a conclusion and rubbed her chin. "I really dig the beard."

"Oh yeah?"

"Yeah, it's hot," she whispered, leaning in for a kiss.

After they kissed, they both looked down at the five-year old child in the middle seat. "Time to wake her up," Harold said. Wendy agreed.

"Hey, sweet pea, we're about to land. You have to sit up tall in your seat."

The little girl yawned as she stretched her arms. After she rubbed the slumber from her eyes, she found her faithful, stuffed reindeer, Gunther. She sat back in her seat and looked at Wendy. "Okay, mommy, I'm ready," she declared in a soft squeaky voice.

After landing and walking through the terminal, the trio made their way to the end of the concourse.

"It's not too bad," Harold said, scanning the line to go through customs.

As they stood at the back of the line, Wendy whispered, "Did Sven pick up the thing we talked about?" She motioned towards the little girl with her eyes.

"He did," Harold said, pulling his phone from his pocket. "I texted him before we left to make sure." Harold looked at his phone. "Oh, Chad sent a text." He opened it up and started chuckling.

"What?" Wendy asked. Harold showed her the text and picture. "Is that his daughter?"

"Nope."

"Niece?"

"Nope."

"Good grief," Wendy responded, rolling her eyes.

"Uncle Chad's funny, huh mommy?" the little girl asked, looking at Wendy with her hazel eyes.

"He sure is, sweetheart," Wendy answered, running her fingers through the little girl's long blonde hair.

After they cleared customs, Harold and his most important ladies looked for Sven. "Doctor Gustafson," Sven said from behind them.

"Yes?" Harold and Wendy said at the same time as they turned toward Sven.

Harold had given up his law practice to pursue his doctorate degree in his passions history and archeology. Initially Chad wasn't very happy with the decision, but came to terms that it had been Harold's dream since he was a child.

"It's good to see you two again," Sven said, shaking Harold's hand then Wendy's. The tall Norwegian looked down at the little girl. "And, who is this little warrior?"

"Hi, I'm Frida," she replied, holding her hand out to shake Sven's hand.

"That's a great name, very strong," Sven said, gently shaking Frida's hand. Sven squinted and rubbed his chin. "We can't have you walking around in the land of Vikings empty-handed." He reached into his bag.

Frida got up on her tip toes, trying to get a peek into the bag. "What's in there?" she asked.

Harold and Wendy smiled.

"You are named after one of our fiercest warrior queens," Sven said.

"Really?" Frida asked.

"Yes. She was well respected, tough and very beautiful. And these were her tools in battle," Sven pulled a small wooden shield and a plastic sword from the bag.

"Wow," Frida said with a huge smile.

"Your mother can show you how to use them," Sven said, handing the items over to Wendy.

"Show me, mommy!"

"Okay, put your arm though the straps," Wendy said, guiding Frida's little arm. "Now, hold it up in front of you like this." Frida held the shield up in a strong posture. "Good. Now hold the sword like this, baby." Frida held them both up perfectly.

"Wow," Sven said. "You're a natural shield maiden." After Frida swung the sword a few times and slew an imaginary dragon, Sven helped Harold with the luggage. "Ready to head to the site?"

"Definitely," Harold responded.

Harold and Sven loaded the luggage into the back of the Land Rover while Wendy and Frida climbed into the back seat. The two men climbed in and they headed north.

"So, how's everything going out there?" Harold asked.

Sven briefly took his eye off the road and looked at Harold. "How did you know about that location? It's an amazing find, Harold!"

Harold looked back at Wendy and then over at Sven. "An old friend told me about it."

"The weaponry we're digging up is fantastic. Swords, axes, shields and they're in great condition. Also, the Viking remains, jewelry, it's astounding," Sven said. "That's one helluva friend," Sven said with a loud laugh.

The city buildings were now in the rearview mirror as they drove through the Norwegian countryside. Harold and Sven continued talking about the archeological finds while Wendy and Frida admired the scenery.

After a thirty-minute drive, Sven turned onto a dirt road. "Not much longer," Sven said. "It's just over this hill."

Sven pulled up next to a large tent on top of the hill. All of them climbed out and stretched.

"Whoa," Wendy said when she caught site of some of the swords on a table under the tent.

"That's just a few we dug up," Sven said with pride. "Come, take a look," he said, walking over to the table.

Harold and Wendy joined him while Frida practiced her newly acquired craft on a poor, unsuspecting tree.

"Take that, dragon," she said, striking the trunk with her plastic sword.

"They're absolutely beautiful," Wendy said, admiring the Viking swords.

Harold smiled as he relived the battle in his head. It was like watching a maestro at work the way Ulfr had carried himself in battle, deadly and efficient, no wasted motion.

"Let's go down to the dig site so you can see the other items," Sven said.

"Absolutely, lead the way," Harold said with anticipation.

The three of them started walking down the hill towards the main site.

"Come on, sweetheart," Wendy said to Frida.

"Coming, mommy," Frida replied, running over to catch up with the adults. She grabbed Wendy's hand and walked alongside her.

Harold paused so they could catch up to him. Wendy gave him a big kiss when she reached him. "This is amazing," she said excitedly.

The four of them resumed the march down the hill towards the main site. Harold pointed at a spot on the field below. "That's where Ulfr jumped over the shield wall."

"Whoa," Wendy replied with a childlike enthusiasm.

The field was marked off in sections with poles and ropes. Scientists from many countries were participating in this excavation. Groups of two to three people were studying the findings in each section. Swords were found in some of the holes, human remains in others.

"Look at this," Sven said, jumping into a hole and delicately picking up a metal object. He wiped some of the dirt off and handed it to Harold.

"No way," Harold said, recognizing the piece.

"What is it?" Wendy asked.

"It's the bracelet of the Earl that Ulfr and his family fought," Harold glowingly answered.

Wendy smiled and caressed his face with her hand. She knew this was a special moment for him.

"You're right," Sven said, climbing out of the hole. "How did you know that?" he asked.

Harold came to his senses. "Uh, I read a lot about it."

Sven continued showing pieces to Harold and Wendy. Frida saw something step out from the tree line, several yards away from them. She turned her head to the side and took a few steps forward. The large gray wolf looked back at her.

"Puppy," she said as she placed her shield and sword on the ground and began walking towards the animal.

Harold and Wendy were so preoccupied with the findings of the dig, they didn't see Frida walk away. She stopped a few feet from the wolf and paused. "Hi, puppy," she said without fear.

The wolf turned around and walked back into the woods. Frida slowly followed it into the forest.

"Sven," one of the other scientists called.

"On my way," Sven said, waving back at the scientist. "Excuse me, I'll be right back," he said to Harold and Wendy.

"Take your time, we'll hang out here for a bit," Harold said.

"How are you doing, sweet pea?" Wendy asked, turning around. Panic set in when she didn't see Frida. "Oh no, Harry. Where is she!"

"Okay, she couldn't have gone too far, babe," Harold said. He became nervous as well when he saw Frida's shield and sword on the ground. He saw the small path she made through the grass leading up to the woods. "She went into the woods," he said pointing it out to Wendy. "Come on."

They followed the path up to the tree line. They entered the woods and began calling out her name. They repeatedly cried out her name as the search for their daughter grew more frantic.

After what seemed like an eternity, a small voice responded to their pleas.

"Mommy, Daddy, I'm over here!"

"This way," Harold said to Wendy. They ran in the direction of Frida's voice.

"Oh shit," Wendy said when she saw Frida standing next to the large gray wolf.

"Whoa," Harold mumbled. "That's the wolf in my dream."

"What are you talking about?" Wendy asked, not taking her eyes off of Frida.

"The wolf on the boat in my visions, that's him."

"Hey Daddy," Frida said, petting the wolf.

"Be careful, baby," Harold said, slowly moving towards them. He stopped a few feet in front of them.

"I'm not scared, he's my friend, daddy."

Harold looked into the wolf's eyes. "Uncle Alex?"

"No daddy, his name is Ulfr," Frida said with a giggle. The wolf softly licked Frida's cheek. She giggled some more. "He wants to show you and Mommy something."

"Oh really, baby. How do you know that?" Harold asked.

"He told me, Daddy. You can't hear him?" Frida responded.

"No baby. I'm sorry, I can't hear him."

"Oh," Frida replied, trying to understand why Harold and Wendy couldn't hear Ulfr speak. "He wants us to follow him," she said, pointing at an opening in the side of the hill. Ulfr stepped over to the cave entrance. "Come on," Frida said, walking over to join her new friend. Harold and Wendy were hesitant to move. "Don't worry you guys, he won't bite."

Harold and Wendy reluctantly joined them. Ulfr pointed at the unlit torches lying on the ground with his nose. Harold picked two of them up and lit them with a lighter. The large wolf went in first, followed by Harold, then Frida and Wendy. Ulfr easily navigated the narrow tunnels.

He's been here before, Harold thought, watching the wolf.

The narrow passage gave way to a large opening. Harold looked around and saw more torches mounted on the wall. Ulfr sat down in front of a massive stone wall while Harold walked around, lighting the mounted torches. Harold could see much better now.

Ulfr motioned for Harold to join him by the wall. Harold walked over and nervously stood next to him. He jumped back when Ulfr rose up on his hind legs and placed his front paws on the wall. The large wolf pressed forward with all his might and the stone sank into the wall. The loud sound of the shifting echoed throughout the cave. Ulfr stood back and dropped down on all fours as the stone rolled to the side, revealing a large iron door behind it.

Ulfr glanced back at Frida. "The key around his neck opens the door, Daddy." Harold saw an old iron key strung on a rope around the wolf's neck. Ulfr lowered his head. "Get it, Daddy."

"Okay, baby," Harold answered in a hesitant tone.

Delicately, Harold grabbed the rope with his shaky fingers and pulled it off Ulfr's neck. He squinted to find the keyhole and found it a few seconds later. He inserted the key and turned it to the right. The sound of the bolt mechanism resonated through the room when the door unlocked.

The room was completely dark. Even before he lit the torch inside, Harold felt that the temperature and air conditions were different than the cave's.

Temperature controlled? he thought.

Ulfr motioned for Wendy and Frida to come closer. They slowly strode over while Harold lit the rest of the torches in the room. He lit the last torch and jumped when he saw a figure next to him.

"Fuck!" he yelled, taking several steps back.

"Language, Daddy," Frida scolded him.

"Are you okay, babe?" Wendy asked.

Harold couldn't contain his excitement when he recognized it. "Wendy, you have to see this!"

Wendy looked at Ulfr. He smiled and nodded his approval. She ran in and saw Harold staring at a complete suit of Viking armor, complete with chain mail and furs on a display rack.

"No way," she mumbled, marveling at the pristine condition of it. She stood next to Harold and studied it. "It's amazing and in mint condition. It looks brand new!"

"It's Ulfr's," Harold replied. "He wore this for battle in my dream," he added with a satisfied smile.

"Wow," Wendy said, gently running her fingers along the chain mail.

Harold scanned the room in awe. He tapped Wendy on the shoulder. "Look," he said as she turned around.

"Holy—" she said.

The armor Lambert wore on the crusades was only a few feet away on another display rack. It was also in pristine condition. They strolled around the room and saw Dietrich's Wehrmacht uniform.

While Harold and Wendy gawked at all of the ancient relics, Ulfr whispered into Frida's ear.

Frida wrapped her arms around the wolf's massive neck and gave him a big hug. "Okay, I'll go get it," she said, running into the room.

Harold kissed Wendy on the cheek. "I'm going to go thank him for showing us this," he said, walking back towards the door.

"Okay, babe," Wendy replied, touching a Templar sword.

"This is fantastic, thank you," Harold said to Ulfr. Ulfr bowed his head and began walking back towards the cave entrance. "Wait," Harold pleaded. "What about all of this stuff?"

"He said it's yours, Daddy," Frida shouted from inside the room. She furiously rummaged through swords and axes looking for something.

Harold looked back at the room and then at Ulfr leaving. "You can't go, I have so many questions," he continued, running after the wolf.

"Come on, baby," Wendy said, holding her hand out to Frida.

"Got it," Frida said once she found the item Ulfr told her about. She ran over and grabbed Wendy's hand and the two of them ran after Harold.

They saw Harold standing at the cave entrance, gazing at something in the woods. Once they reached him, Wendy saw tears in his eyes. She looked over and saw Ulfr standing next to a large female wolf and a small cub.

"It's Frida and their son," Harold struggled to say between deep breaths. Wendy placed her hand over her mouth as tears of joy ran down her cheek.

"Are you sad to see him go, Daddy?" Frida asked.

"I am, baby, but I'm more happy he found his way home," Harold said, wiping his eyes.

The female wolf and their cub turned and walked away, disappearing into the woods. Ulfr did the same, but paused when he heard Wendy's voice. He looked back at them.

"What's that, sweet pea?" she asked Frida.

"Ulfr said you guys would really like it," she replied, handing Wendy a small, nondescript cup.

Wendy looked at it and couldn't contain herself. "Harold, look!" she blurted out.

Harold glanced at it in disbelief. "Is that what I think it is?"

"Yep. It's the holy freakin' grail!" Wendy declared, looking on in amazement. She handed it over to Harold.

"It's magnificent," Harold said, admiring the holy artifact.

He studied it a few seconds more before looking back at Ulfr. Ulfr smiled one last time before disappearing into the mist.

Made in the USA
Coppell, TX
18 December 2024